T0208942

# BEST
# LESBIAN EROTICA
## 20TH ANNIVERSARY EDITION

# BEST
# LESBIAN EROTICA

## 20TH ANNIVERSARY EDITION

*Edited by*
SACCHI GREEN

Published in the United States by Cleis Press, an imprint of Start Midnight LLC, 221 River Street, 9th Floor, Hoboken, NJ 07030

Printed in the United States.
Cover design: Scott Idleman/Blink
Cover photograph: iStockphoto
Text design: Frank Wiedemann
First Edition.
10 9 8 7 6 5 4 3 2 1

Trade paper ISBN: 978-1-62778-154-1
E-book ISBN: 978-1-62778-106-0

"The Further Adventures of Miss Scarlet" by Emily L. Byrne was first published in Forbidden Fruit: Stories of Unwise Lesbian Desire, edited by Cheyenne Blue (Ladylit Publishing, September 2014); "Hot Blood," by D. L. King, was first published in Appetites: Tales of Lesbian Lust, edited by Ily Goyanes (The Liz McMullen Show Publications, February 2015); "Reunion Tour," by Harper Bliss, was first published in Cougars: Five Mature Tales of Lesbian Lust, edited by Harper Bliss (Ladylit Publishing, November 2014); "Smorgasbord," by R. G. Emanuelle, was first published in All You Can Eat: A Buffet of Lesbian Erotica and Romance, edited by R. G. Emanuelle and Andi Marquette (Ylva Publishing, August 2014); "Tears from Heaven," by Jean Roberta, was first published in She Who Must Be Obeyed: Femme Dominant Lesbian Erotica, edited by D. L. King (Lethe Press, July 2014).

# CONTENTS

vii   Introduction • SACCHI GREEN

1   Dust • ROSE DE FER
11   Ascension • LOUISE BLAYDON
20   Tomato Bondage • TERESA NOELLE ROBERTS
29   The Royalty Underground • MEGAN MCFERREN
43   Reunion Tour • HARPER BLISS
54   Hot Blood • D. L. KING
65   Make Them Shine • SOSSITY CHIRICUZIO
72   Tears from Heaven • JEAN ROBERTA
84   Luscious and Wild • SINCLAIR SEXSMITH
90   Smorgasbord • R. G. EMANUELLE
106   A Professional • ROSE P. LETHE
119   Easy • ANNA WATSON
124   Grindhouse • VALERIE ALEXANDER
136   Give and Take • ANNABETH LEONG
149   Mirror, Mirror • FRANKIE GRAYSON
160   The Road to Hell • CHEYENNE BLUE
173   The Further Adventures of Miss Scarlet •
     EMILY L. BYRNE

185   About the Authors
189   About the Editor

# INTRODUCTION

The Best Lesbian Erotica series has a special place in my heart. Twenty years ago, in 1996, Tristan Taormino and Cleis Press published the first volume of Best Lesbian Erotica, and in 1999, to my amazement, my own very first erotica story made it into that anthology. When Tristan Taormino called and said that she loved my piece because it was so *different* I was hooked on the series and the entire genre for good. (Tristan also very kindly pointed out the many improvements I needed to make, of course; I had a lot to learn.) Seven more of my stories made it into further editions of Best Lesbian Erotica, although I got a bit distracted in recent years with editing ten themed anthologies of lesbian erotica myself, eight of them for Cleis Press. Editing this one feels like the greatest honor of all.

Back in 1996 there were far fewer markets for well-written lesbian erotica than there are now, but there were many majorly talented writers with the courage and the burning desire to tell the stories demanding to be told, stories that can still stir your senses and linger in your mind. There have been some changes in erotica over the years, largely in how far we dare to go and how much we think we can get away with, but I still remember stories from those earlier years as challenging as any written today.

The main difference these days is in the quantity of lesbian erotica available, and the numbers of people writing it well. For this 2016 edition there was a superabundance of excellent work, and choosing was a harrowing as well as stimulating experience. Tastes differ, of course, especially when it comes to erotic preferences, so not every story will push every reader's buttons, but for me the writers here make this edition outstandingly worthy of Best Lesbian Erotica's long tradition of sexy excellence.

In the limited space of a single anthology, "best" has to take into account factors beyond any single measurement of quality. An apples and oranges comparison just won't cut it; envision instead, say, peaches...smooth, rosy, rounded peaches...and pears...and maybe the occasional heavy melon. But don't worry. No actual fruit metaphors are abused in this book.

Like Tristan way back then, the idea of "best" for me includes "different," whether it's a brand-new treatment of a familiar theme, a way with language that makes the words dance to an inspired beat, or a plot I've never seen before. Beyond those, each story has to contribute to a balance in the work as a whole, which should include a variety of themes, settings, voices, tone, and diversity of ages, ethnicities and physical attributes. Above all, "best" should mean original ideas, vividly drawn settings, creative imagery, fully developed, believable characters (even if occasionally that requires readers to suspend disbelief for the sake of arousal), and, of course, plenty of steamy sex, with intensely erotic scenes that flow naturally from the story as a whole, ranging from vanilla to BDSM to edgy frontiers that defy classification.

Originality takes many forms. D. L. King melds the familiar tropes of werewolves and lesbian auto mechanics into a character as likable as she is sexy. Megan McFerren's characters take refuge in a London bomb shelter during WWII. Emily L. Byrne's brilliant incarnation of Miss Scarlet seduces a police detective in the NYC subway system. Louise Blaydon's "nice girl" and "bad girl" strike sparks together forming a band on the gritty side of Liverpool in 1961. There are stories with touches of humor, or moments of tenderness, or immersions in the no-holds-barred depths of bondage and the keen pleasures of pain—and now and then all three at once.

What you get, in this anthology, is a seemingly infinite variety of lesbian erotic desires, in all the heat, beauty and power of both our darkness and our light. I'm immeasurably grateful to all these writers who crafted their stories as only each one of them could, and offered them to be included here.

From me, from the writers, and, I hope, from many of you readers, happy twentieth birthday, Best Lesbian Erotica! Birthday spankings may be in order, but be gentle with your paperbacks. With e-books—well, maybe you'd better find a surrogate spankee. Just read a few of these stories with her to warm things up.

Sacchi Green
Amherst, MA

# DUST

Rose de Fer

Alice saw her again just outside of Death Valley. The girl's long, tanned legs were disappearing into the cab of an eighteen-wheeler with Louisiana plates. Dust swirled in the air where the beast had come to a stop and a hairy tattooed arm held the door open while the girl scrambled inside. Alice's heart sank. As she pressed her foot down on the accelerator and sent the gleaming yellow Mustang past the truck, she couldn't help but turn and glance back. But all she could make out was a slender silhouette, like a ghost sitting beside the burly driver.

The radio emitted a burst of static, as though emphasizing the fact that she was getting farther and farther from home. She'd forgotten to charge her iPod and her choices on the FM band ranged from the comical (farm reports and rural phone-in shows) to the frightening (blood-and-thunder preachers).

Signs displayed the distances to cities she never imagined she'd see. Las Vegas. Phoenix. El Paso. Places that seemed so exotic until you were actually on the long desert roads that led to them. Heat made the road shimmer in the distance and the sky was hazy with sand. She had wanted the trip to be exciting, an adventure despite the destination and the reason for it. But hour after hour on the lonely American highways had only served to make her feel small and insignificant. It was a terrifying place, the open road, sprinkled with ghost towns that only underscored the loneliness.

She'd called her sister from the last rest stop. Pauline had been delighted to hear her voice, gushing—again—over how much Alice would love New Mexico, and especially the baby. Alice could hear it howling in the background and the sound made her skin prickle. She resented it already, and Pauline as well for being careless enough to get knocked up by a man who'd abandoned her as soon as the kid was born.

It was nothing new or surprising. Last year Alice had flown out to help her get back into rehab. And the year before that it was some other crisis. Pauline was the older one, for god's sake. Why couldn't she fix her own mistakes? Why did Alice always have to come to her rescue?

But hey, maybe Las Cruces wouldn't be so bad. After all, what did Alice have going for her back in Portland? An office job she hated, in which her days were numbered anyway with the impending restructure. That and an apartment with neighbors who pursed their lips and frowned when she brought girls home, however infrequently that had been of late. Maybe a change of scenery was just what she needed.

*Yeah, keep telling yourself that.*

She shifted gears with more force than was necessary as she pushed the Mustang harder along the dusty highway. There was no point in taking it slow now that she knew the girl had found a ride. But even with the top down and the desert wind in her hair, the majestic countryside only filled her with a sense of gloom.

She'd first spotted the girl back in Oregon, standing on the side of the road, her jet black hair waving and her slender thumb out. It had only taken a second to drink in the beautiful sight of her—her burnished skin, her almond eyes, her elfin features. But Alice hadn't reacted quickly enough, and anyway, she'd been going too fast to stop. For mile after mile afterward, she'd consoled herself with the thought that the hitchhiker probably had a boyfriend stashed in the trees.

But that was then. Now that she'd seen her again, she knew the girl was on her own. Alice wondered where she was going. She didn't look like a wannabe showgirl trying to reach Vegas. In the two glimpses she'd had, the girl had struck her as someone with grander hopes and dreams than that. Someone with intelligence to match her fey grace. Like a ballerina with a degree in physics. Her eyes had flashed in the sunshine and Alice couldn't help but think that they'd made eye contact in the split second it took to pass each other. A connection. But perhaps Alice had just imagined it. Perhaps the girl had just been admiring the car.

Oh, if only she'd hit the brakes! Just screeched to a halt on the side of the road. They could be sitting side by side now, sharing stories to pass the time, getting to know each other. And when it got dark they'd find a motel. The proprietor would only have one room available, and that with a double bed. He would never even suspect what they might get up to. They could claim they were sisters. Although what naughty sisters they would prove to be! They would lie there in the dark, laughing shyly as they explored each other's bodies. Whispering, murmuring, kissing, touching...

Alice stopped the fantasy in its tracks. *Dream on,* she told herself.

She turned the radio on and searched for music, but all she could find was a country and western station. Good old boys crying in their beer over the women who left them for other good old boys, never for someone else's wife or girlfriend. She switched it off and listened instead to the purr of the engine.

The sun was sinking behind her in the hazy sky, but the land was still suffused with warmth. And dust. It was probably time to put the top back up or before long she'd be covered in it. There was a terrifying beauty to the desert. All around her, Joshua trees and cacti spread their prickly arms, like wizards summoning the spirits of the earth.

For a moment she was even sure she'd seen a ghost. Far off in the distance, something was moving, a coiling auger of sand. It was a dust devil, winding its sinuous way across the plain. It moved like a dancer, writhing and undulating. Alice slowed to a stop on the side of the road to watch it, mesmerized by its twisting motion.

The road was empty as far as she could see in either direction and she was alone with the dust devil for several minutes. It was a thing of such strange allure, like a creature from another world. So magical, yet so ephemeral. Even now it was fading, growing thinner. Soon it was nothing but a wisp and then, just like that, it was gone. Tears shimmered in her eyes and she wiped them away, feeling privileged to have seen it.

She started the engine again and adjusted her sunglasses, wondering if she could push on for another couple of hours before looking for a motel. She liked the idea of driving beneath the stars. And if she couldn't find anywhere to stay, she could just sleep in the car. Before she could turn the car back onto the road, a cloud of dust billowed across the highway. And when it had cleared, Alice gasped. The girl was standing there.

At first Alice thought she must be imagining it. All she could do was sit and stare, waiting for the vision to fade. But if the girl was a hallucination, she was a very convincing one. She made her way toward the car, her lithe body swaying gracefully. Then she leaned down on the passenger door, smiling.

"Hello."

Alice could hardly believe the girl had spoken. But she managed to reply. "Hi."

For a moment there was nothing but silence between them. Alice stared in disbelief while the girl merely smiled. It was a sly, lopsided smile, as though she knew something Alice didn't.

"Well? Aren't you going to invite me in?" she said at last.

Alice shook herself out of her daze with an embarrassed laugh. "Yes, of course! Get in, please. I'm sorry."

The girl opened the door and Alice drank in the sight of her. She wore cutoffs that showed off her beautiful legs, and a flimsy linen blouse tied at her midriff revealed both her flat stomach and the pleasing swell of her breasts. She had wound her black hair into a loose knot at the nape of her neck and Alice imagined plunging her hands into it. But it was her eyes that transfixed her most. They were the same shade of blue as the turquoise pendant that nestled between her breasts. It looked like a crescent moon, the points almost touching at the bottom.

"I'm Nina," she said. Then she pulled the door closed and leaned her head back, gazing up into the sky as though she had just dropped from there. Alice could almost believe she had.

"Alice." She didn't know what else to say. It was like being in the presence of royalty.

"Nice to meet you, Alice," Nina said, smiling sidelong at her. After a while she cleared her throat softly. "Well, Alice, are we going anywhere?"

"Oh! Of course!" Flustered, Alice threw the Mustang in gear and winced as the engine protested the rough handling. She got herself under control again once they were on the road. "So—where are you headed?" It was the most banal question, but the only thing she could think of to say. Not that it mattered. If the girl said she was going to Canada or New York, even China, Alice would be tempted to drive her there.

Nina didn't answer. She closed her eyes as the wind blew her long hair out behind her. It moved like a raven's wing. "I saw you before," she said at last.

"You did? Where?"

She turned to look at Alice, her expression unreadable. Her

turquoise eyes gleamed with mischief and delight. "Oh, come now."

Alice nodded, feeling as if she'd been caught spying. "Okay, yes I did. A couple of times." Then she laughed. "That truck driver must have really put his foot down for you to get so far ahead of me."

"I like to go fast," Nina said, her voice silky and insinuating. She kicked off her shoes and raised her legs, putting her feet up on the dashboard.

Alice felt her skin flush with warmth and desire. She stole a glance at her passenger's shapely thighs, letting her gaze travel the length of her legs, down to her bare feet. The toenails had been painted a vivid blue that matched her eyes. There was a tiny jeweled ring on the second toe of her right foot and Alice couldn't help but picture slipping it off with her teeth. Her sex pulsed in response.

Nina still wore a cryptic smile and her eyes seemed to be daring Alice to believe her wildest dreams had come true.

"I like your car," she said, stroking the leather upholstery. Her hand trailed over the seat until it reached Alice's shoulder. Then it moved lightly across her arm.

Alice shivered as gooseflesh rose on her skin. Nina continued her exploration, her touch as delicate as a butterfly's as she stroked Alice's arm, her shoulder, then down her side. When Nina reached her thigh, Alice couldn't suppress a little gasp. The teasing fingers danced for a moment on her jeans, then slipped down between Alice's legs. The car wobbled on the road and Nina laughed, a soft, musical sound. But she didn't stop. She pressed her hand deep into the warm hollow, pushing the hard denim seam right up against Alice's sex.

Alice closed her eyes for a moment, then forced them open, forced herself to concentrate on driving. It was impossible to focus with Nina's hand tormenting her so sweetly. "Please," she moaned, not wanting her to stop. Ever.

Nina leaned over, her lips tantalizingly close. She smelled of dust and honey. "Alice," she whispered, "pull over."

Alice immediately slowed the car and guided it off the road. It crunched to a stop in a rocky patch of scrub between two sprawling Joshua trees. She switched off the engine and closed her eyes, listening to the pounding of her heart in her ears. She was afraid that when she looked again, the girl would be gone, vanished into the sky like the dust devil.

But she didn't need to see to know that she hadn't been abandoned. Nina's fingers were working at the buttons of her shirt.

Alice opened her eyes, taking in the sight of Nina's face, tribal-scarred by the shadows of the desert trees above them.

"You're so beautiful," she managed to whisper.

"So are you," Nina said, her voice low and husky. Her lips grazed Alice's throat, making her shudder. And then they kissed.

Alice melted into the sultry heat of the girl, pulling her close as they mashed their lips together. Nina's tongue sought entry and Alice devoured her, tasting her sweetness. She wanted to stroke Nina's breasts, to bury her face in them, to kiss every dusky inch of her. But she was trapped by the seat belt.

When they finally broke the kiss, she unlocked herself and took Nina's hand. "Come on," she said. "In the back."

Nina clambered over the seat eagerly and curled there waiting until Alice joined her. She arched her back, a wordless invitation. The little crescent pendant dangled enticingly in her cleavage, a splash of blue against her skin. Alice didn't hesitate. With trembling hands she unfastened the knot in Nina's blouse and peeled it open, exposing her breasts. Alice let her fingers trail down the outer swell as they tumbled free, and then took them in her hands, caressing the soft flesh.

Nina shivered and gave a soft little whimper of need, spreading her legs wide as Alice knelt between them. She drew her thumbs across the little stiffening buds of Nina's nipples, and then lowered her mouth to kiss them. Each time she flicked her tongue across one, Nina moaned, her own hands fumbling blindly at Alice's shirt until both women were topless. Alice pushed her breasts against Nina's, pressing their nipples together. The sensation sent jolts of pleasure through her body.

The sky blazed with wild fiery colors, like a Martian landscape. Alice had never seen anything like it. Her hands shook as she unfastened Nina's cutoffs and slid them down. A pair of lacy black panties came next, the gusset as damp as Alice knew her own would be. She skinned down her jeans, eager to feel her nakedness against Nina's.

"Beautiful," Nina murmured, sitting up to look at her lover. Her gaze was so piercing that Alice blushed, fighting the urge to glance away. Nina just smiled again, that sly little cat grin, as she pushed Alice onto her back. She played with Alice's breasts, stimulating her almost past endurance with her fingers, her lips, her tongue. From time to time Nina raised her head for another kiss, angling her knee between Alice's legs as she pressed her mouth to Alice's.

For a moment Alice wondered if she had slipped into some kind of fantastical dream. But Nina lowered her head and Alice felt the girl's lips against her sex, then her tongue. It was hot and wet, and Nina lapped eagerly at the swollen knot of Alice's clit. Waves of pleasure and desire swept through Alice, making her dizzy. Nina swirled her tongue round and round, softly at first and then with more vigor. With her fingers she pulled Alice's thighs wide apart, pressing her mouth hard up against her, sucking her clit and sending little spasms of shock through her.

Alice had been clutching the seat backs, but she let go to bury her hands in Nina's hair. It spilled across the girl's naked back like ink. Alice fisted a hand in the ebony locks, twisting it tightly as she guided Nina into a harder, more desperate rhythm.

Nina obeyed the silent command, nipping Alice's clit with her teeth before soothing it again with her tongue. She varied her ministrations, fluttering her tongue across the sleek folds and then pulling away to stroke them with her fingers. Alice didn't think her legs could go any wider but Nina urged them even farther apart, then slipped two fingers inside her. Then three. Alice had to bite her lip to stop herself screaming when Nina took her clit into her mouth again. The combination of sensations was almost too much to bear. Nina's fingers pushed deep inside her, finding her G-spot as she kissed, licked and sucked the hot little bud that was beginning to throb with the building climax.

All around them the desert winds blew. Dust swirled in the warm air, painting alien designs across the sky. Alice imagined herself lost in the vast openness, a tiny statue made of sand. And Nina was the wind, stroking her, caressing her, slowly carrying her away, grain by grain, setting her free.

At last the pleasure overwhelmed her. It swept her up and under, flooding her body with ecstasy. Alice screamed, loosing a wild cry into the bronzed desert and the sunset sky. Her body quivered and pulsed with each little surge of bliss and she was lost in the moment. She was flying, soaring unfettered in the burning sky, the pulse of the earth throbbing within her. Time seemed to stop as she drifted, euphoric and free.

When at last she came back to herself, Nina was smiling, her eyes like black diamonds. Alice could only gaze at her in wonder for several seconds. She had so much she wanted to say and do, but her mind was a haze of sweet delirium.

"Oh my god," she panted. "That was... I've never..."

"Shhh. There's no need to say anything."

Alice wrapped her arms around Nina and pulled her close. They lay naked and curled together, gazing up at the sky as the colors faded and the stars began to appear. A sliver of moon sailed between them like a ghost.

When Alice opened her eyes it was still dark. The moon had disappeared but there were hints of pale yellow and pink on the horizon. She sat up slowly, blinking around her in a daze. Where was Nina? With a gasp she realized she was naked, wrapped only in her shirt. Her jeans and panties were folded neatly beside her and she dressed quickly, then climbed into the front seat.

Her body was sore, but it was the sweet ache of strenuous sex. Her sex still pulsed with the memory of the night before and she slipped a hand down between her legs and sighed as she remembered Nina's touch.

She peered around at the early morning desert, but there was no sign of the girl. Her heart sank and she pressed a hand against her breast, willing herself to remember only the bliss. There was something around her neck.

Startled, she angled the mirror down to look. It was a turquoise pendant of a crescent moon.

Alice smiled as she revved the engine and guided the Mustang back onto the highway. She floored the gas pedal and savored the rush of speed as she raced toward the horizon. She had made a decision. Her sister could take care of herself for once. Alice had her own life to lead.

And as the sun began to spread its wild colors across the sky, Alice saw a figure standing on the side of the dusty road. Alice slowed the car and pulled up alongside her.

"Going my way?" Nina asked, a playful grin on her lips.

Alice nodded. "Oh yes," she said. "I am now."

# ASCENSION

Louise Blaydon

They met first in a place Annie shouldn't have been. It could hardly have been otherwise—Cat was just that sort of girl, always to be found in places where nice girls didn't venture, hanging desultorily around the docks or walking out with the lads. Everybody knew about Cat. They said she didn't walk out with lads the way another girl might, but walked instead with razor blades under the lapels of her blazer, a tall, upright figure like Hepburn with her long legs in tight jeans, auburn hair piled up messily on her head. She lived in Woolton, a nice bit of Liverpool, with some poor old biddy of an aunt who despaired of her, but her mates were all these lads from Speke and the Dingle, tough as old boots. Cat looked tough, too, bright and sharp and ruthless as a blade.

Annie had seen her often on the bus, and watched from a distance with a mixture of morbid curiosity and awe. It was coming up to '61, now; girls were doing new things, being new people. Whatever Cat was, whatever she did, it wasn't as much of a shock as it might have been ten years ago. But they didn't meet—really meet—until the day Annie took a wrong turn on the way back from dropping off some sheet music for her father, and there was Cat all alone with her spine pressed to the back wall of a blind alley, one foot propping her up, fag smoldering between two fingers.

Annie's gut went cold for a full five seconds before Cat smiled at her. It wasn't safe around those parts for a girl on her own, Cat said. Annie, trotting to keep pace in her buckled school shoes and pleated skirt, refrained from pointing out the obvious. It was quite clear what Cat meant.

She said her name was Catherine, but she said it with a sneer that made the word stupid, ill-fitting to this slim-hipped creature with her fine long nose and russet-colored hair, her man's shirt and imposing boots. Her long eyes were an exact match to her hair, and carefully lined. Annie's fingers ached to draw her.

"What were you doing there?" Annie asked, feeling daring.

Cat laughed and said, "Waiting for my band."

"Your band?" Despite herself, Annie slowed, watching Cat carefully.

Cat shrugged, a loose jerk of her shoulder. "Aye, but they never showed, did they?" She snorted. "Crap, really, the lot of 'em. I've got half a mind to ditch them for someone who can actually bleedin' play a guitar."

The words made their way out of Annie's mouth unbidden, on the back of a strange clenching in her chest, an unfamiliar rush of eagerness. "I can play a guitar," she said. "I'm *good*," she added. Her mother had always warned against false modesty.

Cat snorted, not even a pause for thought. "You're kidding, aren't you?"

Annie frowned. "Why?" A moment ago, she had been wondering what had possessed her, but Cat's immediate dismissal stirred a defensive contrariness in her.

"Well," Cat said, and stopped walking, one corner of her mouth quirking up in a smile. Her hands were in her pockets, where her jeans were stretched so tight over her hips that the lines of her individual fingers showed through the fabric. "You're like a bleedin' choirgirl, love. What's your name?"

Annie frowned. "Anne-Marie. But just Annie, really."

"Well, 'just Annie, really,'" said Cat, in an infuriatingly reasonable tone, "You're hardly the sort, are you? Even if you *can* play the guitar, what'll the lads make of this? You'll be crying over your poor virgin honor, darling." Cat reached out, caught at the hem of Annie's skirt with finger and thumb. Annie jerked, and Cat grinned as if validated, taking her hand back. Her fingers brushed the soft skin on the inside of Annie's knee as she withdrew, and a shiver skittered strangely across the base of Annie's back.

"I know girls like you," Cat said. "Bet you do everything mummy says, don't you?"

"Me mum's dead," Annie shot back, snapping, and it was worth it for the look on Cat's face, the sudden shocked slackness. "And I *can* play the—the f-*fucking* guitar, better than you, I bet."

She turned, primed to leave this strange rude person where she'd found her, but Cat's arm shot out, hand closing around Annie's shoulder.

"Show me," Cat said, soft now.

For some reason it seemed that refusing was not an option.

They never should have been friends. The tight-lipped expression on Mr. Mac's face whenever Cat came round said as much; what was all the more curious to Annie was the fact that Mrs. Smith, the aunt Cat lived with, seemed equally averse to the presence of Annie in her home. Annie wasn't used to being disliked by parents. She was clean and neat and did the ironing for her dad and her brother and herself, *and* still managed to get good marks at the grammar school on the far side of Liverpool. Her mum was dead. Annie had Suffered a Lot, which adults generally cared about. That Mrs. Smith didn't was confusing.

Cat cared. Cat said, "You don't have to do everything for 'em, you know."

They were lying on their backs on Cat's narrow little bed, staring at the ceiling. Annie was wearing a pair of Cat's jeans that Cat had coaxed her into. They were too long in the ankle and Annie felt naked in them, exposed. That something about the feeling was curiously exciting was by the by.

"He's my dad," Annie said automatically, as if this explained everything. "He hasn't got anyone else."

"He's got hands, hasn't he? That could probably manage putting bacon in a pan without your help?"

"I'm his daughter," said Annie, awkward.

"You're not his slave," Cat said. "And you're not his property, either. You're eighteen now, you don't have to do what he says." Cat pulled herself up onto her elbows and eyed Annie's body critically. "Those jeans suit you. Here, take your blouse off, I've got something I want you to try."

Annie didn't bother to point out the hypocrisy. Somehow orders from Cat were not remotely like orders from Dad, who was bald and wrinkled and still thought a Lady shouldn't ever wear trousers. "Dad'll have a fit," she said, fingers going to her buttons.

"Well, we've got a gig on Monday," Cat said, "so we'll have to decide what we're wearing. We can pick tonight and then you can tell Matt and I'll tell the rest of the group whatever we decide, eh?"

Annie paused, faltered, resumed more slowly. The weight of Cat's eyes was palpable, and she felt herself blushing and cursed her pale skin for it. "A gig?" They had never played a proper gig. A gig would make the dream real, even if it remained only a real dream.

"Yeah," Cat said, grinning, and handed Annie a plain black T-shirt. "So try that. See what we think."

\* \* \*

"Has he fucked you?" Cat's voice canted up at the end as if she were angry, although, as far as Annie knew, she had no reason to be.

From the other side of the room, Matt was watching them warily, all angles and bones and stormy brow, long fingers gone white-knuckled where they clutched his guitar. Annie had known Matt since they were eight years old. Matt was her brother, or almost; and somehow it was in this spirit that she let him put his curious long-fingered hands on the prepubescent curves of her breasts when they were twelve, and in her knickers three years later in the McCartneys' living room one night when the house was empty. But she could never… "Matthew?" she hissed, incredulous. "What kind of girl d'you think I am? And even if…" She trailed off. "Matt?"

"He touches you like he's fucked you," Cat said flatly. "Like he's had you." Her eyes were dark and shuttered and Annie sighed, and bit her lip.

Before Cat could make her say it unwillingly, drag it out all wrong, she said, "It was just kids' stuff, that's all. Just to see."

Cat's tone didn't mirror Annie's at all, cutting over her strident and angry. "Oh! Oh, just to see? And that means he's not had you?"

The break in Cat's voice stirred a sudden heat in Annie, blood in her cheeks when she tossed back, "Christ's sake, Catherine, it was only his hands. That's not *fucking*, is it?" She leaned in, said sharply, "It's not *fucking* without someone's prick in you."

Cat swallowed, mouth setting. Her eyes took on a different cast, amused, somehow, as she leaned back and crossed her arms, buttons on her cuffs glinting in the yellow lights of the club. "We'll see about that, McKenzie," she said, and something dipped in the pit of Annie's stomach, hot and strange and good.

* * *

"Watch my folders," Annie said, cautionary. It was half past four; she had arrived home to find Cat skulking on the doorstep, and she was still in her school uniform, blazer and skirt and tie, A-Level Art portfolio tucked under one arm as they moved up the stairs. Useless, staying on to do art, her dad had said, but here she was doing it. More than once, she had questioned whether she would have done it if Cat had not been there that day by the docks.

"You want a cuppa while we write?" Annie asked, glancing behind herself as she leaned the folder carefully against her wardrobe.

"Annie," Cat said. Her voice sounded strange, urgent, and Annie was just on the cusp of asking her what was wrong when Cat moved forward jerkily and cupped her face.

A thousand things rattled through Annie's brain at high speed, looking at Cat like this, her pupils grown black and insistent and her expression curiously pleading. Cat didn't plead. Cat always held the balance of power, and in this moment, Annie realized dully, she did not.

She knew she ought to say, "Cat, stop it," and pry Cat's hands away, take a firm step back. Instead, she said, "No tea, then?" and her voice was low and shaky, her stomach dipping.

Cat's expression wavered, corners of her mouth lifting. "No," she said, and tilted Annie's jaw, holding it captive as she kissed her.

Annie had been warned about Cat, about girls like this. But somehow, Cat had broken through, broken in.

Cat had strong fingers, square shoulders, muscles in her arms. Annie felt soft beneath her when Cat's weight bore the two of them down onto the little single bed and Annie's legs splayed unconsciously, skirt riding up, but it wasn't an unhappy softness. It wasn't the sort of vulnerability she felt when boys touched her like they thought it was their right, and Cat was cleverer, anyway, than any boy; surer, though the look on her face was almost fear. Cat's palm found the inside of Annie's leg, smoothed its warm way up past her knee and then hesitated, suspended somewhere on the soft plain of her inner thigh. Annie reached down, clasped Cat's wrist, and her whole body seemed to thrill, uncertain of whether she meant to stop Cat or to encourage her.

"Let me," Cat said, remembering herself, and ducking her head, mouthed at Annie's lower lip. Annie sighed, chest clenching; lifted her mouth, open, and then they were kissing properly, fully, Cat's tongue hot in Annie's mouth. Her hand shifted, then, sliding upward, and this time Annie didn't interfere, only gasped and spread her thighs when Cat knuckled at her through shamefully damp cotton.

"Please, love," Cat said, running a firm thumb up the center of her, and it wasn't like Matt's tremulous too-eager touch, not at all. Annie rolled her hips against Cat's hand, bit her lip. Her father would kill her if he found out.

"All right," she said.

Afterward, they smoked with the window open, furtive.

"Gonna rain," Cat said, flinging her long legs over the end of the bed and standing, peering out shortsightedly into the street.

"*Cat*—" Annie reached for her wrist, clutched at it, tugging. "Come away from there, you nit; someone'll see you."

"What's to see?" Cat said, but she was smirking as she turned, body long and pale and bare. She moved toward the edge of the bed, stood there with her legs astride and ran a slim hand through Annie's tousled hair. They probably looked horrors, Annie thought. *You look a right clip*, she heard her mother saying.

"Stop it." She spoke as much to the voice in her head as anything, but Cat laughed as Annie caught her around the waist, threw her down onto the mattress. The muscles in her thighs pulled long and taut under the skin and Annie couldn't help but run a hand up them. Cat was dark between her legs and hot and forbidden and it made Annie's throat tight, thinking about it, what this was, what they'd done. Spurred by a sudden impulse, she pushed two fingers together up into Cat where she was still wet from earlier and Cat surged up half-off the bed, gasping and clutching at Annie's shoulders.

"Not the little virgin anymore, are you?" Cat said, voice strained and teasing.

Annie pressed a thumb against her, feeling Cat flutter reflexively, and opened her mouth to speak, but Cat cut her off, put a hand flat over her mouth.

"You're not," she said. "I've had you. You're mine."

Something hot flared in the pit of Annie's stomach, then licked across her shoulder blades. "Oh," she said, and felt suddenly combative, but delightfully so. "We'll see about that," she said, and set to work.

*Girls don't count girls don't count girls don't count...*

But this would count if anyone knew, if anyone saw; this felt like it counted when Annie was pressed to a backyard wall with Cat's mouth between her thighs; this felt like it counted when Cat fell asleep on her shoulder after a gig and a fuck and it *was* fucking, when Cat rolled her hips down hard against Annie's and worked her with her fingers and took her apart with her tongue.

*Girls don't count girls don't count girls don't count...*

But Cat counted; Cat *was* counted, and she'd made sure Annie counted, too. Annie wasn't just a girl anymore. Since she'd met Cat—since they'd played together in their narrow jeans and shinned down the drainpipe in Mansfield Road in the dark; since they'd bunked off school and bickered over lyrics and stretched their hands to shape new chords—she and Cat, they were just people, and that was all.

Cat, Annie thought, was the sort of woman the world needed to meet. The sort of person.

"We've got an offer," Cat said, brandishing a piece of headed notepaper and grinning fit to split her face. "Proper club an' everything, Annie. This is serious."

Annie couldn't help but smile back immediately, but a question niggled at the back of her mind. "Do they *know* about us, though, love? Do they know who's actually in the band?"

Cat tossed her head, pressed her lips together firmly. "No," she said, folding the letter and stuffing it into her pocket, "maybe they don't. But trust me"—and she took Annie's hand—"they fucking will."

# TOMATO BONDAGE

Teresa Noelle Roberts

"Well, that's it!" Julia exclaimed proudly. "Two hundred tomato plants in bondage."

"More than that. I counted two hundred and eight. And we'll have to do it again as they grow."

"But at least we can do that round a little at a time."

I took off my hideous but useful gardening hat and let the breeze ruffle my short, sweat-damp hair. "Damn heirloom tomatoes anyway."

I smiled as I said it. Julia and I both loved the flavor of heirloom tomatoes, and so did our customers at the farmers' market and the local restaurants who bought from us. But these delicious older varieties grew on huge plants that needed to be supported by stakes or trellises, too big to fit into those wire tomato cages found at any hardware store during planting season. We'd rigged up a trellis system out of the scraps and oddments that farmers tended to save—some had come with the place, stashed away by the old couple who'd run dairy cows here until the market gave out. We'd planted the tomatoes on Memorial Day weekend.

Today, they were finally big enough to tie to the trellis, using a combination of string and strips of worn cotton sheets. The farm had come with a supply of those too, forgotten in a linen closet. The sun had moved closer to the western horizon but still beat down hot on this late June afternoon. Both my arms and Julia's sported a yellow-green coat of what I thought of as tomato dust—I'd never learned the technical term for the powdery substance that stained you after wrestling with tomato plants. Julia's forehead was streaked with chartreuse and dirt-brown where she'd brushed away sweat.

She looked amazing. Dirty, but amazing. Defined muscles, built by our shared hard work, in her arms—and, as I knew, her back, abs and thighs as well. The sun caught the reddish lights in her long, dark brown hair. The colors on her skin looked like part of some primal ritual and she could have been the high priestess. No, the goddess.

If I'd look half as good as Julia did covered with tomato dust and glazed with sweat, I'd start painting myself with yellow and brown streaks and spraying myself with salt water before we went out for a night of dancing. Not that we hit the bars of Northampton much between May and September. Occupational hazard of being farmers: our growing-season social life was pretty much nonexistent.

On the other hand, there was a lot to be said for the summer months being the Julia and Molly show. Privacy, work we loved, collaborating with no one but the weather and each other to make our schedules, and did I mention privacy on our isolated homestead?

Privacy, for instance, to slip behind Julia and wrap one of the sheet strips around her wrist. She gasped in surprise, but didn't resist. Not Julia. Instead, she moved her other hand so I could bind her wrists together.

"Shirt off first," I said. Otherwise, what I had in mind wasn't going to work very well.

That command provoked a snort, but her objection had more to do with common sense, which she had in spades, than inhibitions or personal modesty, which she lacked in spades. "What about bugs?"

I grabbed the bottle of citronella-and-herb bug repellant out of the wheelbarrow and brandished it at her. "I'll respritz us both." It wasn't exactly a taste sensation, so I'd keep it away from nipples and other nibble targets, but it should help. And we'd both put sunscreen under our clothes in case it got so sunny we risked burning through our shirts—or in case it got so steamy we indulged in outdoor shenanigans.

"Well all right then." As she answered, she pulled her Fedco Seeds T-shirt over her head and flung it onto the grass path. Her bra quickly followed.

She gave me a second to look at her beautiful breasts, slightly glazed with sweat. Then she kicked off her sneakers and wriggled out of her shorts. No effort to do a sexy striptease, just getting from dressed to gloriously naked under the sun in the most efficient way possible.

That's my girl.

Julia and I have been together for ten years, but I still stopped and stared in appreciation at her delicious combination of curve and muscle, the way the late-day sun played games with light and shadow on her skin and caught reddish highlights in her brown ponytail. Julia rocks the high femme look on those rare occasions when we have a chance to get out and play. I enjoy it when she's wearing heels and an itty-bitty cocktail dress, the kind of outfit that would look stupid on my blockier build even if I had the inclination to dress that way. But I think she's most beautiful to me at moments like this: unguarded, unfashionable, glazed with the sweat of our shared labor and eager for me.

I could have spent hours studying the familiar but always stunning lines of her body and that would have been a great way to while away the rest of the afternoon. But the strip of garish flowered sheet on her right wrist reminded me of my other plans. I shook myself mentally from the pleasant daze that a naked Julia always induces, grabbed her arms and brought them together in front of her. Wrist to elbow, elbow to wrist. A few quick ties with sheet strips and Julia's strong arms were immobilized.

Then, as I'd promised, I applied a light coating of bug spray. Someone who went in for elegant rope bondage might have been appalled by the effect. I hadn't even bothered to pick strips from the same sheet, so several different faded floral patterns clashed on her body.

But her bound arms framed her breasts, accentuating her crinkled dark nipples, so the makeshift bondage was just about perfect. Her eyes were bright, her lips slightly parted in a sensual smile. She stood proud and tall in her makeshift bondage, her long, strong legs slightly parted and her bare toes curling in the dirt.

I ran my fingers across the plump curve at the top of her breasts, dipped into the valley between them. Ran my calloused palms over her nipples until she writhed under my touch. "Please, Molly," she sighed. "I need..."

Julia didn't finish her sentence, but after all these years I knew what she craved when her voice took on that breathy, lost-little-girl quality. I drew back and slapped each breast, not with a farmer's full strength, but hard enough that dusky red hand-prints blossomed on her skin.

"Thank you," she breathed, and then, "More?"

She didn't need to ask twice.

By the third round of slaps, we startled several small birds that had been exploring the mulch for worms. I don't know if it was the smacks or Julia's happy noises that scared them off, but we both laughed as they chirped in alarm and flew away.

I'm neither a classic Dominant nor a true sadist. I don't feel the need to tell Julia what to do—a good thing, because she'd only listen if it amused her—and I don't particularly enjoy administering pain for its own sake. What I enjoy is her reaction to a little pain, a little rough play. Same thing when she feels like having the upper hand. It's not so much the bondage or the spanking I enjoy, although they're fun enough, as her sheer turned-on glee inflicting her pleasant torments.

Now, though, she'd made it clear she wanted it to be my turn on top.

Pinching her nipple hard, I slid the other hand between her legs. She wasn't quite as open as I hoped, so I slapped her inner thighs until she changed her stance. Okay, maybe her stance had been fine in the first place, but I liked the sounds she made when I struck her. Liked the way she canted her pelvis forward to meet my fingers.

And loved the slickness I found flowing from her pussy. "You're drenched." I circled her clit until she ground against me. "Just from that little bit of play."

"I watched you tying the tomatoes," she admitted, "and wished you were tying me up instead."

"Funny"—I pinched the other nipple now, firmly enough that she squealed and jumped—"I went there too. Figured you'd be envying the tomatoes. I kind of was myself, when I wasn't thinking about putting you in their place."

Julia grinned and laughed, though the laugh was half a moan thanks to my busy hands. "You have to be gentle with plants. I don't break that easily."

I'd been planning to lay her down on the soft grass at the edge of the tomato plot and lick that luscious dark plum of a pussy. Maybe even kneel in front of her and do so. We're not hung up on roles, and that way I could smack her ass while I ate her.

But it sounded like my lady needed something more intense this afternoon.

*Challenge accepted!*

I grabbed her bound arms, and pulled her in for a hot, hard kiss. Her lips were dry from the sun and wind, and so were mine, but that didn't matter. Once our tongues twined and the kiss turned possessive and claiming on both sides, I didn't notice the mild discomfort anymore. If I knew Julia, it added an extra fillip of arousal for her.

I thrust one denim-clad leg between her bare ones, and felt her heat radiate into my skin. She ground against me, heedless of dirt, heedless of anything other than need. As she rode my thigh and devoured my mouth, I spanked her. It wasn't the best angle, but sometimes it really *is* the thought that counts. Being bound and spanked, however awkwardly, pushed Julia closer to the edge. Already, I felt her moisture soaking through my jeans.

I didn't want to break away from that delicious kiss, didn't want to lose contact with that wet, eager pussy. Even without any direct contact, my own clit swelled in sympathy, and my cunt began to flood. It would be so easy to shift position, rub against her and get that stimulation I needed. When the time came, I'd explode like an overripe tomato tossed against the wall of a barn.

But I knew how to make Julia even more juicy and aroused. And that, unfortunately for me, involved putting a little distance between our cunts for now. I broke away from the kiss. "Come with me," I said, and was surprised by how gruff and gravelly I sounded. Almost as if it were a real order, not a good idea pretending to be one.

Grasping her bound wrists, I led her out of the tomato field. A little way from its edge was an ancient apple orchard that we were coaxing back to productivity. Even if we weren't getting a lot of apples yet, it was a pretty spot, fragrant with blossoms in May, dappled in green shade in summer, redolent of fruit in fall. We'd set up a small bench back there, a place to rest from our labors and survey our domain.

And sometimes, a place to do other things.

"It sounds like you need a real spanking, not just a few slaps for foreplay. Is that right?"

"Please." She squirmed against her bonds—not to escape them, but to feel them more keenly on her skin. "Please, Molly..."

I sat on the bench, patted my lap and then helped her position herself across it. Enjoying playful spankings was one thing. Falling off my lap and possibly hitting her head on a rock or the bench was another, and with her hands bound, it was a risk.

When she was settled, I ran my hands a few times over the curve of her ass, making her squirm and drinking in the moment. Her skin was soft, warm all over and almost hot where I'd already hit her. Her weight anchored me, rooting me in my desire for her. All around us, summer was rolling over our farm. Birds clamored overhead, and I thought I heard the chattering of a squirrel in one of the trees. Seen through green leaves and tiny apples, the sky was the soft, misted-over blue of high humidity. The air was sultry and smelled of dust and green, growing things. We smelled of dust and green, though those subtler aromas were quickly getting overwhelmed by the fragrance of Julia's arousal.

I took a deep breath, enjoying everything including the keen ache between my own legs.

Then I began to spank her vigorously.

And when a farmer does something vigorously, that's hard-core.

Julia loves pain, but she doesn't take it quietly. She shrieks and screams and yelps and begs for mercy she doesn't actually want unless she uses her safeword (which is *radish*, if you're curious). This little grove of trees, far from the road and the nearest neighbors, was a perfect place for this kind of game. I wished I'd thought of it earlier and made a mental note to look into building a shed out here, something that looked like another small farm building, but on the inside would be a cozy sex-retreat where she could scream and pretend-beg to her heart's content. I doubted we'd have the money for such a project this year, but if we planned ahead, maybe next summer...

Julia's cries and the feel of her firm, supple ass beneath my hand quickly pushed that thought onto the back burner where it belonged. Julia deserved my utter focus. And she got it. I alternated fierce spanking with teasing caresses to her clit and pussy until she was rocking against me, gasping, almost sobbing with need.

If I hadn't been so intent on her, I might have been sobbing with need myself. Her wetness, her scent, her beautiful, red ass, her hoarse noises all conspired to turn me on so much I might have been able to clench my thighs a few times and come.

But why tumble over the edge that impersonal way when I had a lapful of beautiful, wanton woman who'd be happy to take care of my little problem when the time was right?

Her cries intensified. She squirmed more in my lap. "Please... please," she begged. And as I had before, I translated that incoherent plea for her.

"You need to come, baby?"

"Please..." I'd short-circuited her brain so much that for the moment it seemed she couldn't remember any other words. Luckily I had years of practice in the language of an aroused Julia—limited in vocabulary, rich in possibility.

I thrust two fingers into her while I swirled at her clit with my other hand.

She stiffened, convulsed, and came howling. Somewhere down the road, I was sure some weekender from Boston or New York was wondering whether a wildcat or a catamount had found its way into the area.

The noise and the spectacle of her pleasure were enough to make me follow her into orgasm. I closed my eyes, arched back and tried not to drive my fingernails into any part of Julia where it wouldn't be a fun sting.

I'm not as loud as Julia, but I was still glad the neighbors were far away.

Especially when Julia recovered enough that she asked to be untied so she could turn her attentions to me. She ran the strips of cloth between her green-stained fingers and smiled suggestively.

And I found myself saying, "Sure. If bondage is good for you and our tomatoes, it's bound to be good for me."

Like I said, I'm not a Dominant, not a sadist. If you have to put a label on it, I'm a switch, or an experimentally kinky person partnered with someone of similar inclinations. I might be more on the toppy side, Julia more a bottom, but sometimes it was fun to mix it up.

But mostly what I am is a woman in love. And smeared and stained with our farm and with Julia's juices, I couldn't imagine much I wouldn't do to make her happy. Bondage tomato-style? Bring it on.

# THE ROYALTY UNDERGROUND

Megan McFerren

She recalls her father's oft-spoken insistence to keep her chin up, and draws a deep breath. Oily smoke slicks acrid against the back of her throat, and Elizabeth decides that perhaps keeping her chin low might be better. She lifts the collar of her shirt across her nose and holds it there.

The queue shuffles forward, around the side of the Tube station. Toward either side spans Marshalsea Road—toward either side spans destruction. There are no fires she can see, so late in the day, but thick black streams still rise into the air from what once were houses. Despite how often the wireless now uses it, the word *flattened* doesn't seem at all appropriate. To the contrary, the wreckage is tall and incongruous, all jagged edges and unidentifiable fragments of lives that Elizabeth—in a moment of piety—prays survived the raid.

She lowers her eyes again and takes another step down into the Underground, pressing her toes into the well-worn basin at the center of each stair. Countless feet curving even tireless marble: the change that once to her seemed fascinating is now a slow agony of time's movement. What good is marble at all when nightly, bombs destroy homes and shops, streets and churches? What good is there in permanency when if not destroyed outright, it is whittled away by every downward step?

The din of voices seeking shelter beneath Borough station suffices as distraction from the weight of her bag that digs sharply into the curve of her neck. Elizabeth looks away from a crying child whose mother is in no better shape, past schoolboys already at play, too young not to see this all as some grand new adventure. She smiles in spite of her own misgivings. There are whole families here, old people and young couples, shopgirls and even a fiddler, his instrument held against his chest as if it were his progeny.

Chin up.

In their booths, the ticket-takers still on shift watch placidly as the lobby fills. Even in the direst commuter hours, Elizabeth has never seen the station so full. Overhead, the glass light fixtures that once twinkled prisms across the walls have been removed, revealing only the glaring bulbs beneath. Advertisements for shows linger in their frames, promising romance and intrigue at theaters that have been reduced to splintered wood and the rubble of red fabric seats. She shoulders her bag closer to her side, one arm looped over it for her own security as much as for what little she carries inside.

From queue to queue she goes, with no children to console or family members to account for here, when they are all safely north in the Lake District. Barring entrance to the Underground, at the top of every stair stand the shelter wardens. Clipboards in hand as if tallying names for a field trip, their eyes are bright with a curious sort of power. Though the trains have stopped, the clock that marked their arrivals and departures has not, and Elizabeth checks it against her watch. The end of her shift would have been in thirty minutes, nightfall not far behind it.

"Are you in the queue?"

The voice beside her ear startles her, and Elizabeth squeezes a hand over her heart to settle its skipping.

"Yes," she answers, looking past her shoulder to the girl behind her. Dark hair curls loose around a rounded face; freckles are spattered beneath her hazel eyes. "Aren't all of us?"

"Thought you might be taking in the sights."

Elizabeth meets her eyes for a moment more, and turns away to stifle her own amusement. "I've seen enough, really."

They step forward, a sinuous shuffle as the wardens begin to let people down to the platforms, name by name.

"First night?" the girl asks Elizabeth, and she nods.

"Foolish, really. I couldn't bring myself to leave my flat until the one next to it came down. Becomes a bit hard to justify then, when there's suddenly sky outside instead of brick, and all your things have rattled to the floor." Elizabeth shakes her head, and then corrects the bobby pin holding her own tresses back from her face. "Bookcase nearly killed me."

"Better than a bomb," the girl muses. "But not by much."

Another step, and another.

"You're from nearby?" Elizabeth asks. She keeps her voice quiet. It feels out of place to be boisterous when there are so many who seemingly can't control their loud laughter, their cries of greeting, their tears.

"Was," the girl responds, and a step out of turn brings her to beside Elizabeth. "Still am, I suppose, although there's not much of a 'nearby' to return to."

"Oh. Oh, I'm sorry—"

"Everyone's fine," the girl assures her. "No one's been there for weeks."

"You've been here," Elizabeth points out. "Seems unwise."

"Terribly dangerous, you mean. I suppose so. But there's still work to be had, and once the Germans are done, I'll find some-where to stay. See what's still standing."

She smiles, a crooked sort of pleasure in the corners of her eyes, and Elizabeth watches her with dismay. "That's so morbid."

"It is, and so perfectly suited for these trying times," she says, lowering her voice in mimicry of the nightly news. "We must all carry on, chin up and all that."

Elizabeth blinks, and surprises herself with a laugh.

"Welcome back, Catherine," intones the sprightly old shelter warden, smiling enough to raise her glasses higher.

"Good evening, Mrs. Blankenship," she answers. Her arm slips through Elizabeth's to tug her forward. "I've brought a friend tonight."

The wire frames lower. "Have you, then."

In an instant, Elizabeth relives every dubious look she's ever gotten from her parents, her teachers, her friends and peers. Before she learned to stop saying that she wasn't interested in boys, before she learned to say that she was simply waiting for the right one to marry, before she learned to nod and feign attention when they told her to just find a nice man and settle. She forces a smile.

Chin up.

"Elizabeth Dyer," she says, rising to her toes to peek at her name jotted down beside Catherine's. The arm around hers remains, long enough that Elizabeth has time to resent the blush rising uninvited to her cheeks.

"Welcome to Borough Tube, Ms. Dyer. You'll see that we've marked off areas for sleeping, others for personal needs and food preparation—"

"I'll show you," Catherine whispers, before turning a sunny smile to the warden. "Thank you, Mrs. Blankenship. I'm certain the accommodations will be lovely as ever."

Elizabeth is tugged along briskly, nearly dropping her shoulder bag as they bound down the stairs. Catherine's arm slips free, palm skimming Elizabeth's elbow, to seek her fingers instead and lace them. Elizabeth's breath stops, her heart ceases to beat for an instant and she finds she can no more stir them to life again than she can tug her hand away. In matching dresses of dreary gray wool, bare legged without stockings available to them, they appear as much to be sisters as anything else. Perhaps they are, of sorts, and Elizabeth only notices the looks they receive because so few are sent their way.

"You're mad," she decides, as the girl turns to face her.

"No," Catherine answers, canting her head. "I'm familiar."

"Overly familiar."

"I can be unfamiliar instead," she offers.

There's a challenge in the words and Elizabeth crooks a brow. Catherine, to her credit, seems entirely genial either way. They only met a staircase ago, but the girl is unfairly charming, breezy as if they'd met at the park rather than hiding beneath it. Elizabeth wonders what might have happened had they encountered each other anywhere else, the long uncertain looks they might have shared before lips caught coy between their teeth in knowing grins.

Elizabeth thinks distantly of the flat where she kept her own company, but with room enough for two, and her cheeks burn. In answer, she simply shakes her head. Catherine's smile bounces back, broad teeth peeking beneath rosy lips, unmarked by lipsticks long ago rationed.

"Elizabeth, is it?"

"Yes. Just that, not Liz or Beth or anything," she answers, fighting down a smile that begs to appear in response to the other girl's enthusiasm. "It's nice to meet you, Catherine."

"So it is. Queens, the both of us," she grins. "The royalty underground."

Where she goes, Elizabeth follows. Tiled walls bend overhead, growing smaller down the darkened railway tunnel. Already large families are staking claim to parts of the platform; already those who came alone are instead making their bed upon the tracks. Elizabeth's steps slow to watch an elderly couple taking tea together from a thermos and a single cup, shared between them.

"I've my own, if you'd like some," Catherine offers, giving a nod for Elizabeth to keep with her as they continue on.

"Tea?"

"It might have a top-off of scotch in it."

"Might have," Elizabeth repeats.

"Definitely does," corrects Catherine. "Here, just through."

They take a turn to a maintenance hallway, its door removed to allow for better ventilation. No sooner is the corner turned than the beehive hum of voices from the platform is dimmed, and Elizabeth sighs her relief before she can put any mind to propriety.

"Oh," she sighs, slumping to the wall. "That's glorious."

"Best to get here early if you like it," Catherine says. "Most assume it's off-limits."

"Is it?"

"Might be," she shrugs. "But once the platform's full they'll start to push in here if you're not already in."

Elizabeth's throat tightens when she tries to swallow, and a stark realization slips tense between her ribs. It's hard to breathe here, harder still to imagine that people like Catherine have spent weeks in this place. She slips lower down the wall to sit against the cold cement and lets her bag slip from her shoulder.

Chin up.

"It's awful, isn't it?"

"You just said it's glorious," Catherine reminds her, wide smile gentling. Elizabeth looks away, bringing her knees together against the ground, legs tucked beside, and she sits in silence as Catherine unpacks her things.

"It's what we make of it," she adds after a moment more. "No different than being above ground. A flat, a townhouse— any one of them can be a misery, depending on how you see them. Who's there with you."

"Any bed is better than the ground."

"Is it?" Catherine asks. Their eyes meet for a moment, and she says again, "Depends on who's there with you."

"Fair," agrees Elizabeth. She turns the backs of her fingers against her cheek, to cool away her blooming blush, and sighs. "Do you mind if I—"

"Not at all."

They sip together in the relative quiet of their nook, a shared cup passed from hand to hand, lips pressed to the metal made hot by the drink within. What the tea doesn't heat, the scotch does, and when neither is sufficient to distract from the blur of voices on the platform outside, their fingers brush.

Elizabeth draws a breath so sharply Catherine blinks at her, and a feline smile curves her lips. A dubious look is sent her way, and Elizabeth snatches the cup back with a prim lift of her chin. It does little to hide what both know, when they share another gaze and it lasts a beat longer than it should. It does little to distance them from the pleasant distraction, meeting someone so much like themselves in such an unlikely place.

"What do you do?" Elizabeth asks. She rests the edge of the cup against her mouth and notes with amusement how Catherine watches the motion.

"You mean when I'm not kidnapping pretty girls down into the Tube?"

"Unless that's all you do."

"I don't make a habit of it," says Catherine. "I'm a secretary when the lights are on."

"And when they're off?"

"I make do," she says simply, and Elizabeth laughs before she can stop herself.

"Is that what this is?"

Catherine grins and sets her back against the wall. She toes off her shoes, the leather cracked and peeling, in a way they wouldn't be were they not all practicing dutiful austerity. She sets bare feet against the wall where Elizabeth sits; Elizabeth mirrors the movement. Their knees settle together, calves brush opposing thighs softly enough to shiver them both, and neither withdraws.

"I used to work at the cinema," Elizabeth murmurs. "I liked being able to finish my shift and take in the films, until newsreels started to take as long as the movies. Endless reels one after the next, until I couldn't stop imagining what it must be like to be beneath the planes and hear their hum overhead. By the time the film started, all I wanted was to be back in my flat with a novel, somewhere else."

She declines the cup again, fingers fanning politely, and Catherine caps what's left of their scant supply.

"I feel like the war came to find me instead," she says. "I feel responsible."

"For Hitler?" Catherine laughs. "I'll have to ask you to leave my corner if you are."

Elizabeth shrugs, watching the dim lights glow across the tiles overhead. "Maybe if I'd kept going, it might have—oh, I don't know. It doesn't make any sense, does it?"

"None at all," agrees Catherine.

With a sigh, Elizabeth drags her bag nearer. She starts to unpack as Catherine had, a pile for the clothes she could fit inside her rucksack, a few books loved into pale covers and rounded edges, a few squares of chocolate left from her rations. Her hand brushes against the plastic lens of her gas mask, but she lets it stay, for now. "What do we do—?"

Above ground, a siren agonizes, and their eyes jerk to the tunnel ceiling.

Chin up.

Rising and falling, far slower than the stuttering inside Elizabeth's chest, the alarm's strange, tuneless melody winds in languid wails. Not the steady pitch of all clear as the city shrouds itself in darkness for the blackout, but a warning, cyclical and endless. It matters not a whit that she's in a shelter, that earth and scaffold and cement surround them—the pressure in her chest grows, splintering outward and then suddenly drawing in, hollow and cold, into a void at the bottom of her belly. Expansion and implosion.

Catherine's hand startles her nearly to tears, the touch too hot compared to the cold cement on which they sit. Without thought for anything but desperate comfort, their fingers pass clumsily over and squeeze, then release. Somehow, Elizabeth manages a laugh.

"You think I'd be used to it," she murmurs. "It's quieter down here, at least."

"I'd be more concerned if you *were* accustomed to air raids," Catherine answers, matter-of-fact.

"Like you are?"

"No."

With pensive movements, Catherine bundles their spare clothes together to create a serviceable pillow wide enough for both. Elizabeth follows her lead now as she did before, and they slowly stretch to lying face-to-face. Only a meter away, on the platform outside their little hall, a man speaks in animated voices to distract his distraught children with a bedtime story.

"They don't shut the lights off down here, in case we need to evacuate," Catherine says. With a shrug, she peels back her overcoat, a sprightly pale gray, and drapes it over them both. Warm vanilla scents the lining, a perfume worn enough that now the fabric holds its ghost.

Beneath this makeshift blanket, the world seems very small, consisting entirely of the other. Even Elizabeth's anxiety seems shrunken to a nervousness of nearness, pressed so close as this. She's certain her respiration is too loud, her heartbeat audible, and though she tries to settle both, it only seems to make them more conspicuous. Her body echoes in her own head, drowning out the drone of sirens and voices. Her throat clicks when she swallows.

The roar becomes deafening when Catherine sets cool fingers against her cheek, and Elizabeth lets break another inappropriate laugh.

"I'm not easy," she whispers, never mind that no one can hear them, never mind that her proclamation is weak and meaningless, rendered childish in the circumstances.

"No?"

"No," Elizabeth says. She licks her bottom lip between her teeth and presses them against the tender inner skin. She isn't easy. But the ground has been uprooted from beneath them by the endless anticipation of an end that has yet to come but could at any moment. A direct hit from overhead would see them gone in a flash, and what good was living if done in dread? What good does reputation matter then?

"No," she says again, inching her shoulders closer across the cold floor. "And I'm not going to kiss you lying on the platform of a Tube station."

She does anyway. Just a touch, lips curling together, whiskey-warm. Catherine's hand spreads against her cheek and she tucks a curl of hair behind her ear. No more than that. Only a kiss.

Their noses brush together when they part.

"We shouldn't do that again," Catherine considers. She's scarcely able to keep the smile away, teasing a fine fan of lines beside her eyes. "It would be too easy."

They do anyway. Through the stiff wool of their dresses, their breasts cushion together. They seek the other's hand blindly to press their palms and twine their fingers so tight that the squeeze of bones brings a kind distraction from the dizzying gathering of their kiss. Whatever moves them, moves them deeply, opens each to allow the other within, tongues tracing teeth and breath whispering loud against flushed cheeks. Like kissing for practice in secondary school, like kissing for intent in secret pubs, Elizabeth unfurls with familiarity, if not with Catherine than with the idea of her.

Damn the war and damn the blitz. Haven't girls like them always survived?

Parting just for air, just for a laugh passed between their mouths, it is Catherine now who watches with surprise from the sudden intensity and Elizabeth who narrows her eyes in amusement. They heat quickly beneath the coat above them, breath heavy as hands softly work down the slopes and rises of the other's breasts, hips, legs. Catherine curls short nails sharp against the outside of Elizabeth's thigh, no tights to keep skin from skin, and a shiver ricochets up Elizabeth's spine.

"I'm not going to keep touching you," Catherine warns.

"I hope you won't," answers Elizabeth. "I intend on keeping my hands entirely to myself."

"Good."

"Good."

"It would be a very questionable choice if they were to stray," Catherine adds.

"Where might they stray? I'll keep them to myself."

"You know how idle hands wander. My blouse, perhaps," she whispers, dark eyes flashing bright in dim light dispersed through the fibers of her coat.

"You could lose a button that way," notes Elizabeth, as carefully she pushes one free of its mooring. And then another. And then another. "If you lost a button down here, you'd never find it."

"It's good you'll restrain, then."

"Yes," Elizabeth says, as she fills her hand with the weight of Catherine's breast. No tedious lingerie to mangle through, most women having given up the attempt in favor of outward patriotism and personal enjoyment. There is only tender skin and pebbled nipple, hardening beneath her thumb, before Elizabeth ducks her head to bring it past her lips with a whisper: "God save rationing."

She fills her mouth and hollows her cheeks, and stroking her tongue against the firm nub, sucks lewdly loud. The sound is lost, between their sighs and their shifting, beneath the blanket they've made and beneath the earth itself. A curse escapes Catherine when Elizabeth relents with a cooling sigh to seek the other in turn. She tangles one hand in Elizabeth's curls and skims the other beneath the hem of Elizabeth's skirt. Up high to the band of her knickers, over a pointed hip, the thin material tugged tight when she finds the coarse curls of hair between her legs. Catherine tightens her grip at the back of Elizabeth's head just enough to catch her attention, and part her lips damp from around Catherine's breast as she lifts her eyes to Catherine in quiet question.

Breathless, her fingers tease across the soft swell of Elizabeth's belly, and Catherine whispers, "I'm going to—"

"You are," Elizabeth says, asks, hopes, pleads.

"And you?"

"I will," she answers, searching between Catherine's eyes before a wide smile breaks free. "Even though we should not," she says, hoping the whisper of laughter doesn't sound as desperate as it feels. "Even though you should not pull harder—"

Elizabeth gasps, words cut short and neck arching as Catherine snares her hair tighter, her body rigid in rough delight. She stretches a leg to twine with Catherine's, palming her breast and scraping her nails down the plush swell of it. Their breath shortens between them, so loud now there is no mind for sirens or conversations outside—no world at all outside the one in which they rut in furtive, schoolgirl secrecy. Twisting Elizabeth's panties aside enough to push her fingers further within, her wetness slicks hot against Catherine's touch, their gaze settled together, near enough to kiss but only brushing their lips, slow, soft, panting.

Catherine rubs her palm flat across Elizabeth's mound, setting her hips into motion. Curling forward to meet the subtle ridges of Catherine's hand, its delicate textures made luminous in detail against her lips when Elizabeth is so sensitive already. She moans low when her hair is released, and sets her brow to Catherine's shoulder. One by one, fingers press deeper, parting her wide, and a brush of contact where Elizabeth stiffens snaps her hips rigid.

"Not there," Elizabeth whispers, a laugh caught on her words. "Definitely not—"

Catherine's fingers still against her clitoris, holding a steady pressure, enough to dizzy her. A wry smile fills her words as Catherine asks, "Not there? Well."

"No, I mean that—I mean, I don't mean that," says Elizabeth, helpless, smiling so wide it nearly hurts as their game falls apart between them. "Please don't stop."

"You mean it?"

"I mean it."

Her moan is muffled by the coat over their heads when Catherine rubs firm and fast against her. Slick fingers glide quickly across her hardened nub, and Elizabeth tries to stop her limbs from trembling but fails, wonderfully fails, instead wrapping her hands in Catherine's open shirt to catch herself. She can do little more than grind down against Catherine's hand in response, little more than whimper hitched sounds that rise, quickening, like a warning of her own imminent fall. The world shifts beneath her, and whether it's from this tender barrage or the bombs up top, Elizabeth hardly cares. A shiver cinches her body tight, twisting deep in her belly, so taut she can't draw breath, until all at once the roar in her ears detonates. She uncoils, breath and body and beating heart. Expansion and implosion. Squeezing her thighs against Catherine's hand as dampness trickles down her leg.

Undulating with the shock waves, Elizabeth's hips hardly slow, and she couldn't stop them if she tried. Catherine's patient fingers spread her open farther, seeking lower, and Elizabeth parts her legs so that heated fingertips caress her opening, for now simply stroking.

She should feel some sort of shame about this, she imagines, meeting women in holes underground, ones that are strange beyond just being strangers. Is she so desperate as that, to ride to release the first woman to offer easy company and an easier laugh, with boisterous talk of royalty as they lie tangled together?

Perhaps she is. Perhaps the time or place has made her so.

When Catherine kisses her again, her worries fade. One must always find a way to keep one's chin up.

# REUNION TOUR

### Harper Bliss

You're a cocky little thing up there. The way you wriggle your ass—I can't wait to stripe it with my belt. I watch you from the side of the stage. If this were a festival in Europe, my band would be headlining, but here in our home country, yours gets the number one spot. I'd be lying if I said it didn't smart a little. I may have to take that out on you as well. It's a win-win, really, the way you bat your lashes—your head twisted up to me—when my hand comes down on your flesh, always defying me to give more. And, when it comes to you, I never fail to have more to give.

You shimmy to the edge of the stage, lifting your arms high above your head, giving your fans—and me—a glimpse of your pale, taut belly and the little silver ring driven into the delicate skin above your belly button.

"No one will know what it means," I said, when I arranged for Lisa to administer the piercing. "Only the two of us." Now, every time you flash it, every single time you bare this glittering symbol of whatever we have between us for the world to see, something pierces me, too. A wave of something I don't wish to define washes over me. I'm old enough to recognize it instantly, but still foolish enough to deny it.

Because you drive me crazy, make me feel things I haven't felt in years. Not even taking the stage again, after a nine year hiatus, flanked by Tommy and Matthew and Sam, my brothers in arms since 1981, affected me in the same way as the first time I saw that glint in your eyes. All it took was one glance, and I knew.

You flick your head to the right, momentarily pinning your gaze on me, and the whole motion thunders through me, leaves my panties drenched. Speaking of, you're wearing a pair of mine underneath those leather trousers—the ones that hug your ass so sublimely I need to catch my breath every time you present your back to me on the stage.

"Please allow me to present to you the next big thing," my manager said. "The Harriettes." You were obviously their leader, the way you hung back a bit—the way I learned to do all those years ago—to allow the others to shine during moments of lesser importance, like being introduced to a band long past its prime.

"Oh my god," your bass player giggled. "We are such huge fans. You are our biggest inspiration." It sounded a bit rehearsed, what with her not even having been born yet the year we broke through. You appeared smarter, more composed, shrouded in that cool sort of silence that no one can take issue with.

When we shook hands, though, I detected the slightest hint of sweat on your palm, and when you met my gaze, I knew. I'm old enough to know.

You take your first of many faux-modest bows. After five months on the road together, I know your routine by heart. I can only imagine the adrenaline coursing through your blood right now. Not that it doesn't still happen to me, but the years have taken away the highest highs. I've learned to put it all into perspective more, to see the long run—the endgame. But I hope you're enjoying this moment because it truly is glorious. Unencumbered by self-consciousness, lifted up by the incessant roar of the thousands of people in front of you, that one moment you sang and strutted your ass off for over the past forty-five minutes. The higher your high, the more you'll want me after.

You and your band members exit the stage, walking right past me, as usual. The first time it happened after we'd been together, it hurt a little bit, but I never held that against you. It would be like holding being young against youth. You're pumped, ready to go back out there, to soak up whatever precious minutes of adoration you have left after your gig. Yet, for all your bravado, your magnetizing stage presence, and your—admittedly—raw, powerful vocals, you never let it go to your head.

"I need you to do this to me," you said, the first time. But I didn't need you to tell me that.

I wait patiently, glaring into the bright lights of the stage, the corners of my mouth lifting spontaneously as the people out there scream your name, scream for you to come back. Our own fans, like ourselves, are older now, and rarely call for encores in this unbridled, shameless, self-effacing way.

When you shuffle past me again, it's as though I can smell you. Your sweat. The state of arousal you've worked yourself into during your set.

"I'll be there," I whisper to no one but myself. "I'll be there when you come down."

And I am. After you perform two more songs—The Harriettes' first hit, "Boyfriends," and that cover you and the girls always insist on playing of our 1986 song "It's Not Me"—I rush to my changing room. At least, due to my status as new wave goddess of the eighties, most venues, even festivals, easily grant me my wish for my own dressing room.

If I wanted to, I could count down the minutes it takes from the applause on the other side of the stage to die down until you knock on my door. It never takes more than five—just enough time to exchange some high fives with your bandmates—and you always knock.

"Come in," I say, in my most earnest voice. No time for smiles just yet.

You close the door behind you and lean against it, sinking your front teeth into your bottom lip. Already, the first pang of hunger, of blind, delirious lust, shoots through me. To this day, it's still unclear if you chose me or if I chose you. Perhaps we just chose each other. Perhaps, in that long first glance we shared, we saw what we could mean to each other.

As per our ritual, your back stays glued to my dressing room door. I forbade you months ago to lock it. I get up from where I was sitting—a rather dingy couch, unworthy of the backstage of a festival of this standing—and, slowly, take a few steps in your direction. The first thing I always do is unhook my belt and slide it, loop by loop, from around the waistband of my jeans.

Your eyes catch on it and your teeth sink deeper. There's a twitchiness to your demeanor, a desire so great it shines through in every tiny movement you make. You don't know this, but I feel it, too. It burns through me now, and destroys me a little every time you close the door behind you again, every time you leave. But I don't think of the pain that is to come, because this moment is not about my pain. It's about yours.

I fold the belt in my hands, enjoying the soft caress of the well-used leather. Your eyes are glued to it. They always are. The way you can never look me in the eyes beforehand, and how you make up for that afterward by sending defying glance after defying glance at me, as though you've just survived the greatest ordeal, the biggest challenge of your young life, always floors me a little, makes the crotch of my jeans go damp in a flash.

"Take them off." As much as I admire how you look in that pair of leather pants, how they cling to you the way I sometimes want to, time is of the essence.

You kick off your shoes first. You know I want you totally

naked, not a scrap of clothing lingering on your body to protect you from what I'm about to give you. I don't go for anything less than complete surrender. Your top is next. I'm glad you're not wearing that old faded T-shirt with my face on it. I hate to see myself crumpled on the floor like that. As usual, you're not wearing a bra. And I didn't even ask you this time. The sight of you, naked from the waist up, only clad in those leather pants—and those large, snaking tattoos that crowd the skin of your arms and shoulders—makes my pussy clench around nothing.

I don't need to take a picture of you this way. I carry this image with me throughout the days. I see it in the morning just before I open my eyes and before I drift off into sleep at night. When did it become all you, I wonder? When did the balance I sought so hard to find in my life tip in your direction?

You don't need me to tell you that I love you. I'm about to show you, again.

I arch up my eyebrows, indicating my impatience. Pants. Now. There's no need for me to say these words, either. Your hands are pushing the leather down already, and it reminds me of the leather slipping through my hands, sliding through the gaps between my fingers. Leather and fingers. All you need. Maybe you should write a song about that?

I nod my head in the direction of the couch and, once you've kicked both your trousers and panties off your ankles, you patter over there. And, in moments like these, I do wonder where I get the strength to not push you down and ravage you immediately. This display of youth, so present in the smoothness of your skin, the agility of your muscles, the ease with which you take the pain…it shouldn't be for me to touch anymore, but the fact that I can, that you let me, arouses me even more. Because, for as much as you sometimes claim this is a one-way street and complain that you barely get to touch me, this—you naked, at my mercy—is about all I can take. Any more of you, and my old, abused heart may give up.

You know the position and you take it without direction. Your ass arched up high, your torso folded over the armrest, your legs spread wide.

I swallow hard as I approach, and take a moment to behold your beauty. The skin of your behind lost its smooth, silken, youthful unblemishedness after our first night together. When—not if—you ever decide to take another lover, I will always be there with you, and her. I push the thought from my mind, but don't move just yet. I let you stew, anticipate, melt.

Then, at last, I run the side of my belt along the curve of your ass. Up and down, and I need to activate all my willpower to not let my fingers follow the track of the belt. The need to touch you is so much stronger than on any other given night. Perhaps because this tour of ours only has a few more stops left. Because I can feel something is about to end, again. I guess I'll have to write a song about this, too, in veiled terms, and with a contradictory upbeat melody.

I love you, all of you, but when it comes to your body, I love your ass most of all. It's so firm and bouncy—and those tan lines. I told you once, in an unguarded moment, that I found tan lines inexplicably sexy. You've been working on yours ever since, resulting in a white *V* tapering downward along your crack. It makes me feel things I haven't felt in years.

When I let the belt drop off your side, I can hear you inhale. Your body tenses with anticipation, but I wait. Just a fraction of a second, just to throw you off guard a little. I know that you know why I do this, and you adjust yourself accordingly. You make it look as though you relax, while, between your legs, that clit of yours must be thumping—screaming, like mine. Like your fans earlier. Like my heart when you knocked on the door.

The leather cracks down on your pert flesh, but you take the first blow with a solemn sort of dignity that baffles me. All throughout this secret affair of ours, so many things you've done have amazed me. But this, this stoicism, as though it's the most important part of what we do, has thrown me for a loop the most.

I don't hold back, and a pinkish stripe has formed on your skin already. Time to paint your other cheek. The room is silent, apart from the threatening, exhilarating whoosh of the belt, your intake of breath and the stifled moan you expel as the leather touches down again.

As much as I admire how brave you are in the beginning, it's the unraveling of you I crave the most. You make me work for it, though—although *work* is hardly the correct word.

"Is this what you want?" I ask, as I pause and, with the slightest of touches, run a finger over your crack, all the way down to your soaking wet pussy lips. "Is it?" I insist.

"Yes," you groan, your voice a flimsy echo of the one you use onstage.

I let my finger skate all the way down to your clit, and I revel in how ready you already are, but we both know we haven't even started yet.

My finger retreats and I look you over. I can't tear my eyes away from your behind—my biggest prize. I think of the platinum records I amassed over the years, all of them now stashed away in my basement at home, and I consider how none of them ever gave me as much satisfaction as leering at your blushing ass on display right now. My trophy. All mine.

You don't know all of this yet—and, sure, you remind me of me when I was your age, and I didn't have a clue either back then—but fame is always fleeting. And, most of the time, the highs barely erase the lows. This is not how I think about our romance—because, no matter the practicalities and our silently agreed upon arrangements, this *is* romance. I can ride this high for as long as it takes.

Still, today I need to ask. I need you to tell me what is going on in that pretty little head of yours, underneath the mask of your face, which I can't see right now because you've pushed it into one of the couch cushions. At the previous stop of this tour, I had my assistant buy a T-shirt with your face on it. I was amazed to learn that they even still made those at first, but you and your band members always claim to be so old school, so I guess it makes sense.

I run the belt over the curve where your ass meets your thigh, again and again, marking the spot where it will land next.

"What are you thinking?" I ask, giving voice to my own weakness. It's the first time I've asked you this question. I slap the leather lightly against the exact spot I will paint red in a few seconds, so you know I mean business. When I discovered that spot, when I found out how it made your knees buckle when flogged from the right angle and with the right amount of pressure, my clit throbbed so hard beneath my jeans, I wanted to plunge my free hand into my pants and come for you. Only, it wouldn't have been for you. So I didn't do it.

You push yourself up from the cushion you have your head buried in and crane your neck, finding my eyes, but you don't speak.

*Whack.* The leather finds the spot and, instantly, tears well in your big brown eyes.

"Tell me," I say, but don't wait for a reply. Instead, I let the belt come down again, striking you hard in the same spot again. Every time my wrist flicks, a bolt of lightning runs through my blood.

"Tell me how much you want this." I lock my gaze on you, but your eyes close and open, blinking in that mute despair I can't get enough of. You try to open your mouth, but I don't give you the opportunity to form words. I rain down my belt on your tender flesh, that perfectly shaped mound that I will caress later, after you've gotten as much as you can take.

"Look at me." I put as much threat in my voice as I can muster because your head is starting to drop down again, your forehead almost touching that cushion again, and I need to see your face. You can't speak, so I need to get my answers there.

Time for my fingers to take over again. I let them travel along the fresh stripes on your flesh, before directing them to your puffed-up pussy lips.

Immediately, you moan while your pupils dilate. "Fuck me," you whisper. "Please."

I draw my lips into a smirk—the one I used for the picture on that T-shirt of me you love to wear. "I think you need a little more."

"I—" Your breath stalls as my finger slides a little deeper inside. Just the tip. Just to tease. "I want you so fucking much," you manage to say after my finger has retreated and is riding upward again, smearing some of your juices onto the most sensitive patches of your skin.

"I can tell," I say. This is always the moment where I could go further. Where I could tell you all the reasons why you don't deserve it yet, but I don't believe enough in them myself to try and fake that speech for you—although I'm quite sure you'd like the tone of voice in which I would deliver the words. "Not yet, baby," I say instead, my own bravado quickly starting to crumble. Because the courage in your eyes undoes me, more so than other times. Do you feel it, too? Do you feel that this is ending? Or do you have a master plan? The tabloids would have a field day, and believe me, my front page days are over.

I surprise myself with the force of the next slap on your tortured cheeks, but there it is, that glint in your eyes I've been waiting for. You set your jaw, as if to say that, as of now, you can take all I've got. Perhaps you know that I don't have that much left, but I don't think you do. I think you're all in. I think you want more and, this time, I'm happy to oblige.

I let a few well-aimed slaps come down near the highest curve of your ass where, I suspect, it hurts the least. But you don't need time to breathe, I can see it in your eyes. *Is that all you've got?* they seem to say. And this game we play, this charged silence between us, the quiet we fill with our own thoughts and needs and fantasies, they leave me gasping for air more than you are at this point. And I hope that you can read it on my face as well. How much I need this. How much I want you.

It's this unrelenting want that undoes me in the end. I witness my own unraveling instead of yours. I drop the belt to the floor and position myself behind you. Even glancing backward at me, your neck twisted in an awkward, possibly painful position, you have the nerve to sink your teeth into your bottom lip. *Yes. I give in.* I don't say this out loud, but I know you get the message loud and clear.

Roughly, I spread your legs as wide as they can go, and I lock my gaze on the wetness in front of me. How long will you last this time? I know you fight hard to make it last; I can feel it in the way you twitch, and in how you push your body away from me when I fuck you, but I always find the spot.

Your beauty floors me again, the smoothness of your youth, the swollen pinkness of your sex. You're no longer looking at me, and your back curves gently into the exquisite nape of your neck—the exact spot I'd like to sink my teeth into right now. But I'm not about to fuck you because you're young, or because it makes me feel younger. I will fuck you because you're you, and uniquely so. Mandy Harrison—you once said your mom was a big fan and named you after me. Front woman of The Harriettes. The girl who can't get enough of my belt on her ass. Sometimes, onstage, when you're watching me, I touch the belt and the heat that rises from my core is so great, my voice drowns in it for an instant. But no one ever notices, except you.

I plunge three fingers inside of you at once. I know how wide you can stretch, and I slide in easily, lubricated by all the juices you started producing the moment you took the stage. I fuck you. I feel you. I watch your back arch inward, your head tilt sideways, your ass slam against the palm of my hand.

Today, you don't resist. Your body meets me as I thrust, so

I give you a fourth finger, filling you up—as close as I'll ever come to disappearing inside of you. I watch the reddening criss-crosses on your ass, admiring my work, as you grind your way to orgasm. My fingers are but a tool for you now, or perhaps that's what you want me to believe. Our romance is certainly an unspoken one, as much to the outside world as in this cocoon we're in now.

When you come, the groan you utter is close to your singing voice, that raw, deep howl that has all the critics raving, but this particular guttural inflection of it is reserved just for me. "Amanda," you whisper, out of breath. "Fuck, Amanda." And the way you say my name is like I've never heard you say anything else. It's your code for *I love you.*

"I love you, too," I murmur, but only to myself, as I let my fingers slide from your wetness, and drape my fully-clothed body over your bare back, embracing you as though I never want to let you go.

# HOT BLOOD

D. L. King

There's nothing I love more than the freedom of running through the woods out behind the old mill on a bright, moonlit night in the fall. I don't mean to be so specific about it, really. I mean, don't get me wrong; I like just being out there—day or night. I like running, walking, or just lying in the pine needles under that big old mamma up near the ridge. Yeah, propped up against that trunk, at sunset, you can see clear out to the big water. A person could get lost in her thoughts out there with the breeze and the smells and the sounds of all the little critters. Yeah. But still, there's something about the freedom of racing along, the moon tracking you, the wind in your hair, the smell of the fallen leaves and pine needles, the feel of the ground springing up beneath your feet to push you along faster.

Faster.

When I come back to myself, that's the only thought I remember: Faster. But now...I gotta go to work.

I rolled out of bed and jumped in the shower. Why do people say that: "I jumped in the shower"? More like I plodded across the room, wishing I could crawl back under the covers, and crawled into the shower. But I slowly woke up under the water pulsing out of the showerhead. I don't know why people like "gentle rain" showers. I need a good strong pounding to wake up, much less to feel like I'm getting clean. Before I knew it, I was out the door and kick-starting my bike, then off down the mountain to civilization.

"Hey, Van, I got a good one for ya," Larry called as I walked around the side of the garage. I saw a powder-blue Porsche on the lift.

"Okay. But first I'm going to the Bluebell for breakfast. I'm not all the way awake yet. I'll be back soon," I called.

"Oh, you think this is for you? Nah, this ain't for you. This beauty is all mine."

"Whatever you say, Larry." Larry could do anything with American metal but he hated what he called "all them foreign jobs." That's one of the reasons he hired me; that, and I am a kick-ass mechanic.

I walked into the Bluebell and saw that my usual table was occupied. I took a seat at another two-top away from the windows. Too bad. I like being able to look out when I'm eating, but the cute little redhead who'd stolen my table almost made up for it.

"Morning, Van." Tory turned my cup over and poured the best coffee in Washington State into it. "Sorry about your table. Want your usual?"

"Yeah, thanks. No worries. It's not like my name's on it or anything. 'Sides, I'm kinda likin' the view from here."

Tory chuckled and went off to place my order with the kitchen and I took a few more surreptitious glances at the redhead. Definitely from out of town. I knew all the locals and I would have remembered seeing her. I wondered what she was doing here. We're off the beaten path and not really a tourist destination. Maybe she had relatives in the area.

I cut into the beautiful, rare steak Tory placed on my table, and it bled into the hash browns and eggs just the way I like it. I'm a carnivore. Well, I suppose I'm an omnivore, to be absolutely correct. I eat other things, like vegetables and breads and fruits too, but I like meat, the bloodier the better. The redhead was eating dry toast and what looked like yogurt, fruit, and granola mix, along with one of those big cups that held the fancy coffees, like the lattes and such. Nope, I was a meat and black coffee woman. But she sure was cute.

I laid waste to the plate and did everything but lick it clean in about fifteen minutes. I took my time to watch the view, but I had to get back to work and find out what was wrong with that pretty sports car. I left money on the table and called a goodbye to Tory and went back to the garage, fueled and ready to work.

Turned out the Porsche needed a fuel pump. Wouldn't be a hard job, but I had to send to Seattle for the part. It was going to be two days before someone could schlep one out to us because—off the beaten path. I was changing the oil on a Toyota when I heard Larry talking to someone who sounded upset.

"Hey, Van, can you come out here?" Larry called.

I walked into the office, wiping my hands on a rag, to find the redhead there. She looked about to cry. "What'd you do, Larry?" I said.

"What? Nothing. She's just... Can you just tell her about her car?" I looked at him. "The Porsche."

"Oh, sure. Hi, I'm Van, uh, Vanessa. That's a sweet car. It's not too bad; just needs a new fuel pump. I called our supplier in Seattle and they're sending one out. You visiting relatives? Got somewhere to stay for another couple of days?" Her mouth dropped open.

"No. I was just passing through. I really need to get home today. Is there a car rental place in town?"

"Sorry," I said, "we're not much more than a wide place in the road." She looked at me, and I thought she was going to cry.

"But don't you worry; I'm a top-notch master mechanic. I'll do your baby right. Meanwhile, there's a motel that's not too bad, up near the freeway entrance. Larry could run you up there." I looked at him. "Right Larry? I only have my bike with me, or I'd do it."

Larry said, "Sure."

She still looked really upset, but she knew there wasn't anything else to be done about it.

"What's your name?"

"Oh, sorry," she said. "It's Katharine." She reached out her hand and I grasped it. The lady had a strong grip—and something else I sensed. "Is it okay if I hang around town for a little while? Maybe even explore a little bit? I wasn't planning on staying overnight."

"Sure thing. Come on back whenever you're ready."

We were pretty slammed in the garage the rest of the morning. Beauford may be in the middle of nowhere, but that's just it, it's in the middle of nowhere, and Larry and I are a class act as far as fixing cars goes. Miss Katharine wandered back about lunchtime with a few bags. I told Larry I'd take care of her and went to get his keys.

"Hey, Katharine," I said. I stretched out my arms and neck when I hit the patch of sun just in front of the garage doors. "I'll get you settled. How about some lunch first?" She looked a little wary, but our eyes met and she bowed her head slightly and nodded her assent. "All right then. I'll take you to the pub. We're just a little kink in the road and we don't have much, but the Bluebell's got great breakfasts and the Star's got the best burgers I've had anywhere."

I settled us into a booth in back and ordered a bacon cheeseburger, rare, with all the fixins, a plate of sweet potato fries and a Coke. She started to order a salad, but I put my hand on hers and said, "Remember? Best burgers. And I know you aren't a vegetarian."

She looked at my hand and then at my eyes and said to me, instead of the waitress, "Okay. Cheeseburger, medium-well, with lettuce, tomatoes, and onions and a Dr. Pepper. " The waitress wrote her order down and went off toward the kitchen.

When we were alone I said, "Look, you're in the best place you can be. You can't get back to Idaho today, that's a given, so you should make the best of a bad situation. I'm not going to take you to the motel; I'm going to take you home with me."

She pulled her hand back. "No! I can't go home with you. No. You don't know…I'm not like… You don't know me…"

"Katharine, I know you." I looked into her eyes. "I know who you are and I know what you are and I know we're the same. I have a house up the mountain, away from everything, on the prettiest piece of woods you'd ever want to see. There's nothing out there but some deer and coyotes. There's the occasional cougar and maybe, if you're lucky, you might see a black bear or even a moose, but there ain't any people. So you'll be safe."

Her eyes filled up. "How—how'd you know?" she whispered.

"How'd you not know? That's the question. Honey, I could smell you a mile away. Like calls to like." She looked at me like I was speaking a different language. "Is this—wait a minute. Is this your first season? No, it's not your first; you were way too intent on getting out of town. But it's not long, is it?"

"It's my fourth time," she said, tears and defiance in her eyes.

"But surely someone must have helped you through it all. I mean, the one who turned you…" I could tell that was something worse than a sore subject.

"No one. There was no one."

"I'll take care of you. Don't you worry about it. Let's get out of here and go home, where we can talk." We walked back to the garage to get the truck. I let Larry know I was taking Katherine but that I'd be back before closing to swap out his truck for my bike.

"Hey, Van, don't do anything I wouldn't do," he said.

"Larry, you old dog! It ain't like that." Well, it wasn't. She was in a bad place and I'd never take advantage like that. But that didn't mean I hadn't thought about getting closer. I thought I'd like that—if things were different. That red hair, those green eyes and that tight butt? Oh yeah, I'd like that—if things were different.

I think the farther up the mountain we went, the more relaxed she got. She knew I was taking her out to the back of beyond. The story wasn't a good one. The creature that turned her ran off. She never knew who the human counterpart was and she had to find out about being a wolf on her own. I can't even imagine. If Stokeley's brother hadn't found me and brought me to the pack, I don't know what I might have done. But Katharine had no one to tell her the lore or show her the ropes. All she knew was that she'd become a monster and her only thought was to get away from people.

After she told me what she knew about her changing and I told her my story, she asked me the hard questions—the ones even I didn't have answers to.

"No, I'm just not the pack kind of girl. It made me feel too confined. I don't like living by other folks' rules, you know? I guess I'm just a lone wolf." I barked a laugh. "But I can find out about any packs in your area. You know, get you involved with the people out your way. I think, when you're new to shifting, a pack is good. It's good to have folks standing behind you, teaching you, helping you, running with you. Well, you'll see tonight. We'll run together and you'll see what that's like."

I carried her suitcase up to the guest bedroom and told her to make herself comfortable. "I'm just going to switch Larry's truck out. I'll be back soon. It'll be a few hours yet before sundown."

When I came back, she was sitting on the couch in a pair of really short cutoffs and a white A-shirt, feet up on the coffee table, watching the news on TV. She was all legs and arms, long

HOT BLOOD

and lean and so sexy. I cleared my throat and she looked at me.

"So, here's the thing, you probably already know this, but I don't know what you do and don't know yet—but it's easier to get naked before you change, because, you know, if you don't, your clothes will get all ripped up. I'm just sayin'."

She looked at me and said, "Yeah, I figured that one out last month. Sometimes I can be a little slow."

"And it's a good idea to be outside before the moon rises, you know, so your house doesn't get torn up."

She nodded, "Yep, makes sense."

"I also built an outside shower off the back deck so you don't track in mud 'n', you know, stuff." I felt so nervous talking to her. She was just watching me from the couch, looking like she was taking it all in, but I was practically vibrating with nerves, not to mention starting to sweat. It didn't make any sense. I was telling her normal, everyday stuff, well, if you're a werewolf, but still, nothing earthshaking. I was beginning to feel like I could fall into her green eyes and take a swim, though. Maybe that had something to do with it. I cleared my throat again.

"So, a shower, that's a great idea. Maybe I'll do that when I get home," she said. "Are you okay? You look a little, um... Would you like some coffee? I made some while you were gone."

"Sure, great," I said. "Just black."

She walked into the kitchen. "I know. I was watching you at breakfast."

Huh, no shit. I took the proffered coffee and sat down on the couch with her. I was afraid it'd be too weak, but it was good—nice and strong.

We chatted a little bit and she put her hand on my thigh. "I just want to, um..." She gave me a quick peck on the lips. "I just wanted to do that before we, you know. I just wanted to, you know, to thank you for what you're doing."

I reached the short distance to her neck and brought her face back to me, and my lips locked on hers. She tasted so sweet.

My heart began to pound, and my blood sang in my veins. It had been a long time since I'd had this kind of reaction to a girl. Since before the change. I hadn't let myself get close to anyone since, hadn't wanted to. But maybe it was because I just hadn't found the right person. Or it could be nothing. Wolves mate for life, but we aren't above a nip and tumble with a sexy piece of fluff, either. So maybe she was just a sexy piece of fluff.

While she was busy kissing me back, I reached under her shirt and snaked my hand up to a breast. She wasn't wearing a bra and her tit was just the right size for my hand. I gave it a nice, friendly squeeze before rubbing it in circles, pressing harder with each rotation. When she moaned into my mouth, I squeezed and dragged her to her feet so I could slide the shirt up over her head and throw it on the floor.

We gazed at each other as she unbuttoned her shorts and I slipped my T-shirt off and threw it on the floor with hers. As she slid her shorts and underwear down those long legs, I quickly undid my jeans and reached down to untie my boots so I could kick them off and finish getting my jeans off. I couldn't stop looking at her. She was gorgeous: long legs, curvy hips and a round, killer ass, and those teacup breasts. My mouth latched on to one while I took hold of her hip and let my other hand run up and down her back, sliding over that luscious bottom.

Her hands were busy too. On my breasts, on my back, on my ass, until her fingers snaked their way into my pussy and I jumped. I half-pulled and half-dragged her outside. I could feel the moon, and I knew she couldn't sense it yet. The moon on full days made me practically writhe with sexuality. It's the hot blood. Usually I sated the desire with hunting and the very literal taste of hot blood coating my throat and running down my chest, but tonight I wanted to sate it with something else.

The moon took her and she fell to the ground and screamed. The scream morphed into a howl as she became more wolf than human. I watched her change because I knew she didn't have control. It wasn't the same for me. I could wait until the last minute and change almost instantaneously. So I waited and watched and protected her.

Once her metamorphosis was complete, she lay on her side, panting, tired, I knew, from the pain and physicality involved in the change. I caught her eye and flipped a switch in my brain and almost immediately my wolf stood before her on four legs. She started to get up but I knocked her back down with my paw and growled deep in the back of my throat. She had to know who was in charge. She didn't know where she was, and I had to keep her safe. That meant she had to be submissive to me.

She backed away on her belly and raised her rear end, keeping her forelegs on the ground and her head down. What a beautiful creature. She was red, blonde, and black brindle and still had those amazing green eyes. I remember the human world when I'm a wolf, but not in the same way I do as a human. I think the same holds true when I lose the wolf. I can remember what it felt like, but not in the same way I do as a wolf. I do, however, remember everything I did, which can sometimes be a blessing and sometimes a curse because it really is the blood I crave.

I rolled her over onto her back and gripped her throat loosely in my teeth, not to hurt her, but to seal her submissive bargain. She closed her eyes and whined and I licked her mouth, sniffed her paws and her sex. Then, stealing a little lick, I bounded back a foot, allowing her to rise. She understood, got up and shook herself, then followed me as I moved off into the woods. I trotted out slowly until I knew she'd have no trouble keeping up, and then we were both racing the moon. And the feel of the wind and the scent of the earth fed an intangible sense of freedom. But now I was hungry. Hungry for meat and bone and blood.

I stopped and listened. I smelled fresh water and a decent-sized animal ahead, maybe fifty feet. We crept closer and sighted a single beaver in the creek. Circling round behind it, I waited for my moment and pounced, going for the throat. The beaver screamed and twisted under me and managed to bite my shoulder before I could get a good grip on him. Katharine jumped into the creek to help with the kill and got smacked with the creature's tail, but together, we managed a fairly easy kill.

Dragging the carcass up the bank, we blooded ourselves and feasted on the meat. After drinking our fill of water a little ways up the creek, we viewed the moon through the trees. I began to howl and she joined in. Nothing feels better than a full belly and a good howl. We ran a bit more and finally settled down to sleep off the meal.

I awoke the next morning to find myself spooning Katharine, my legs entwined with hers, her head resting on my arm, and my other arm thrown protectively over her. Waking up naked in the woods is usually a bit disconcerting. I have to say, it's much nicer waking up naked in the woods, wrapped around a beautiful woman. I nuzzled against her neck, and she awoke and stretched in my arms.

"Good morning, sleepyhead," I said. Somehow I knew that a kiss would be a bad idea, at least until we'd had a chance to get home and cleaned up. I seldom strayed very far from my house on full-moon nights, so we didn't have far to go. Both our bodies were streaked with mud and dried blood. It's never bothered me before, but I wasn't sure how Katharine would react. I had no idea what she'd done her first four months as a wolf and I was afraid, based on her propensity for salads, that she'd be upset, but she seemed to take it in stride.

We showered together and, once clean, lingered under the water awhile. I kissed her and then spun her to push my chest against her back. Wrapping my arms around her I hugged her.

"What did you think of last night?" I asked. "Was it better, worse, or the same?" I ran a hand over both breasts and down her belly.

"I liked it. I've never enjoyed my wolf before." She leaned back against me, resting her head on my shoulder. "It was easy—nice—running with you. I've killed before but hated every moment of it. I didn't hate it last night."

My fingers played in her pubic hair as she talked.

"I could sense your joy and, I don't know, maybe it was catching. All I know is I had a good time last night and I never thought I'd be able to say that. So thank you."

My hand continued down and I split her pussy open with my finger and began to rub. She jumped back and yipped.

"What's the matter?" I asked.

"Well," she said. "I'm sore, there. Really sore, you know?"

I knelt down in the shower and gently parted her folds. Her lips were swollen and puffy and her sex was red and a little raw looking. And then I remembered.

"Oh, man, I'm sorry," I said.

"No, it's okay," she said. "I remember it was really nice while you were doing it."

I remembered spending I don't know how long, but a long time last night, licking and nipping at her sex. It could have been hours. It was like I couldn't get enough of her and her hot, tasty blood. And now we were both paying the price. I started to laugh. What else could I do? I turned off the water and grabbed a towel for her and one for me.

"Well, fuck," I said. "I guess that means no sex. I'll try to remember not to do that again tonight."

"Oh, I don't know," she said. "I kinda liked it." She took the towel and got quiet.

I did too. We'd be together for this moon cycle, but then her car would be ready and she'd be gone and I knew I'd miss her. "Idaho isn't really all that far from here, you know," I said.

She turned to me and smiled. "I was thinking the same thing."

# MAKE THEM SHINE

## Sossity Chiricuzio

I sense a trail of sparks wending through the crowd and right up near to me in the shape of this lanky genderqueer, now standing just within my peripheral vision. I've seen them before, exchanged some clever banter, noticed walk and hands, and now, in this dim light, I notice the crowding in their back pocket. At least two, maybe three hankies, and as I try to figure out what complex signal code I'm seeing, I realize that they are watching me. I fight the impulse to look away—sometimes shy just won't serve.

They turn to the left, throwing a better light on the pocket, and look back at me. I confirm that the lightest one is indeed mint green—even in femme-friendly Portland, a mama hankie is rarely seen—and my teeth and cunt both clench down for a moment in anticipation. Distracted as I am, it takes a moment for the other two to register: a black-polish-stained length of cotton rag, and a vintage men's handkerchief with *brat* stitched in the corner in crooked black script. I've hit the lotto of good karma payoff, and I don't even try to hide my grin. Practically made to order.

I know enough about them to know that my brain, the word-smithing twist of language in my mouth, and the sharp edge of my wit are all equally as compelling as the rich flesh I inhabit. But make no mistake, the flesh does compel. It is a mama fullness I carry: soft covering firm covering an iron will, and the tenderness to apply it. I am not simply curvy, I am fat: dove's breast, summer-thick peach, rolling hills, high-moon fullness, white-capped waves, lush as cream on your upper lip, fat. Shameless.

This boy wants it, wants it all.

Wants to grab hold of, be restrained by, be denied, be granted, sink deep into this flesh. Burly and sensitive and carrying a scent of my own pheromones, welling up in my sweat where it beads between my breasts. To lay a finger, tongue, cock, just there... to push in and nestle and rub and claim, for a moment, their strength and softness. The boy is gazing at me, and it's all in their eyes—a dark heat, a trembling shiny lust. I know well this primal craving for a sacred initiation, untrampled by all that is thrust upon us in this "civilized" world as we strive to survive childhood. It's a bone-deep desire for the potent combination of sweet safety and sacred whore—a loving, terrifying gateway to self.

I have survived my own mad scramble to become who I am; shed demons rather than parts of my body and found a deep source of power in loving the flesh that is, rather than the flesh that "should be." I can take all that fury, all that sorrow, all that joy, all that pleasure—pour it on, pound it in—let it roll through me, and out, and cradle you there, both of us purified by the flood. This is the promise my gaze returns, my body offers. This is what the boy seeks; and we make our way through several dances, in and out of an energetic, flirtatious conversation, down the dark city streets, up to their room, into privacy and the peace before the storm. The practicality of our discussion is in no way formal, occurring as it does in the midst of the surrender of jackets, scarves, buttons, zippers, personal space.

Between kisses that defy time we move to the bed, laying out ground rules, off limits and safewords, and then lose ourselves in the play of tongue and lips, and the transfer of power, playfully, slowly, into my hands. Sweet boy, brat boy, their mouth full of words sugared and salty, pushing me to take them down—not disrespect, but rather a high-wire joyous grace and eagerness for the tumbling fall...down and down and opened wide. Were I actually the big cat I feel like at these times, I'd fasten my teeth into the back of their neck and shake them into submission. As it is, I bite down into shoulders, jawline, flickering soft kisses across the indents of my teeth as they shudder and release that belly-deep breath of softening, and give over to me.

In this moment, they are mine. Mine to reward, to punish, to fill, to leave empty, to spread myself over and slide against until we're both shaking. Mine to leave alone, eyes closed, hands empty, waiting. Mine to gather up and cover with kisses, nibbling them into giggles and whispered pleas. Not to possess, but to celebrate, and revere, and witness and bless. To gaze into eyes glistening with the tears of being fully seen, and root that deeply in their heart. This is sacred work we'll do here, together. It's also scorching-hot sex, flesh swollen taut and aching, vulnerable and full of need.

I have them pinned beneath me, hands wrapped around biceps, feeling muscles tighten and hips jerk against me, uncontrollably. I can feel the hard length of cock pressed against me through denim and black satin—the combination of textures and slickness making every movement rich torment. Their fingers are tangled in my fishnets, pulling, testing, trying to creep farther up my thighs in something approaching subtlety. The crook of my eyebrow disabuses them of any such success, and sends a mingled look of glee and frustration chasing across their face as they move hands away and flat against the bed, as previously instructed. Having already gone through this cycle three times, I decide atonement is in order.

I pull away, leaving them aching and widespread on the bed, and gaze down long and deep, until a flush begins to spread across their cheeks. They'd like to look away, but that would be a mistake, and they sense it, and freeze. I stand up, straighten my clothes, walk across the room to the easy chair in the corner and seat myself, taking my time. They've turned their head to maintain the line of sight, but otherwise remain still. Fast learner after all. I look down at my boots, scuffed and dusty, look back at them, and give the command:

"Show me your skills, boy."

They scramble to their feet and begin to gather supplies, then kneel in front of me, quickly arranging bottles and cans in an orderly fashion around them—everything in its place. Reaching out to pick up my right foot with a practiced move developed on many a Saturday leather bar night, and then stopping, midair. They look up at me and ask permission.

"Mama, may I polish your boots for you?"

With my nod they lift my foot up onto their thigh, and begin working with quiet certainty. There's plenty to do—these boots reach up high, with laces running through hooks from ankle to knee. I feel their fingers tremble as they brush against me while undoing my tidy bow, but their movements stay focused and precise. They lean in close, for just a moment, not quite laying their cheek against my calf, and I feel leg muscles tense under my boot sole. The interplay of energy through the leather is like lightning to the brain, and the groin—we're both heady with it. My other senses are heightened as well. I feel the skin of my body tightening in pleasure; I breathe in the scent of polish and sweat, and the sound of the laces slipping loose fills the room.

My boots are an extension of me. They radiate power, queerness, the ability to take me across my own mud puddles and climb up into trucks and carry me home from wherever I go. They are sturdy enough for mosh pits and gravel roads and woodland sex marathons and hours of marching. They make my short skirts subversive and mark me as not easy prey. They are a clue about me, a signal to other outlaws, the ones who work with their hands, on their feet, the ones that stand strong in the face of adversity, and claim their perversity as a blessing, and a right. By kneeling at my feet and polishing my boots as a conscious act of service, this boy is honoring all of that. Smoothing out the scuffs of wrestling and traveling and carrying and dancing, and rubbing those memories into me all the deeper. They are caressing me through my supple armor, and the channels open wide, uncanny nerve connections sparking into life and I feel every stroke like it's inside my skin. This delectable boy is deep into the give-and-take of oil and leather, using the strength of arms and shoulders with every stroke.

They move my foot up against their chest, to better work it into the grooves in the leather, slipping their fingers slow and firm into every cranny. The press of my foot into their chest is almost involuntary, as is the breath that hisses in between their teeth. The sound of it brings up both my tenderness, and my desire to inflict pain. I back off, just a bit, and they lean into me like a wall, or a strong wind, seeking that solid press, asking for it...and why not press down, just a little, like praise, like a thank-you? I bend my knee, bringing them closer to me as my skirt lifts, ever so slowly. They fight to look only at my boots, and keep steady hands for the task, though their breathing grows more ragged. What we both want is to fuck, but first to wait, and wait just a bit longer, until it hurts. Until someone begs for it. I am determined it will not be me, and bend my knee further. They are now fighting not only a desire to fall upon me, but also gravity, and the grip of greased hands, and mutter something under their breath.

"What was that?"

"Nothing..."

I look at them, eyes narrowing.

"Nothing, Mama."

I grab a handful of hair at the back of their head, and pull, just a bit.

"I just, I just said...I just said you were mean."

I let go of their hair and straighten my leg in the same movement—sending them sprawling backward for a moment before the grip I have on their shirt stops them short. Before they can find their balance, I come out of my chair and push them all the way to the floor, fast and gentle, and whisper into their ear:

"If you get one drop of that oil on me, it's game over, so you better not move."

I straighten up, look down, see that their arms are stretched as wide as possible and feel a wicked smile forming on my face. I begin to run my hands over my breasts, stroking and cradling them, pinching my nipples and rocking, just a bit. Their face is a study of lust and vexation and I chuckle to myself as I slip my hands into my bra, and then remove it entirely. I lean over, pressing myself against their chest, and slide one hand down, under my leather mini, and inside my panties. They can feel my fingers slipping over and over and around my clit, and they arch, just a little, trying to move against me, entice me. I simply gaze down at their face while I get closer and closer to coming, feeling trembling beneath me, wanting, left wanting...and I come, small guttural sounds escaping as I bite down on their shoulder. I raise up onto my knees and slowly, finally, open their jeans, release their cock and reach for a condom.

They are shaking, working so hard not to grab me, and I take pity, and forgo further teasing in favor of sinking down onto their cock, hard and fast. They thrust deeper than I think possible, using only their legs and back, and I come again, quicker than intended, and see a look of victory in their eyes.

We tease back and forth, moving with and then against each other, establishing and breaking rhythms—until I begin to bear down hard and circle, using my hips to pin them and grind. Their breath comes shorter, legs quivering beneath me, and as I lean in and devour their mouth with kisses, they come, buried deep inside my cunt. I brace myself on my forearms and keep kissing them, mouth and eyelids and forehead, tender and passionate, and lick the salt tears that trickle down their temples. I put my mouth close to their ear, and whisper again: "Sweet boy. Good boy. You've still got another boot to do…"

# TEARS FROM HEAVEN

Jean Roberta

Sheets of rain are pouring down the picture window through which I'm gazing at the emerald green of a well-kept lawn. If hail follows this rain, my flowers will probably be beaten to the ground, but I have no inclination to rush outdoors to cover them with plastic. I have already lost something infinitely more precious to me.

I notice my reflection in my hall mirror just as lightning gives my skin an eerie blue-white glow. My cheekbones look carved from marble, and my lips look taut, although apparently fuller than ever. My brown eyes, looking at themselves, show more clarity than I remember seeing there, as though they had been washed by tears. I haven't actually wept.

I can see the curve of my breasts under a black cotton T-shirt. My Black Watch tartan shorts hug my small waist and my hips like mourning wear for the weekend. For an instant I see myself as the Widow Athena Chalkdust. Absurdity can be comforting.

In my summer break from teaching, I have become unusually domestic. I've been avoiding the university for days at a time, and I hope that my colleagues in the English Department can accept my absence as well as I can survive without office gossip and rivalry. Until two weeks ago, I was content with my garden, my books and my pets, human and animal.

Didrick, my able-bodied former student, was my gardener and maid-of-all-work. I watched her planting flowers and vegetables in receptive soil, and the symbolic implications of her work did not escape me. She washed the silk sheets of the bed where I took her, and where her diligence left me wet and fragrant. My poor *protégée* has never learned to write a solid sentence, but she poured her energy into becoming a one-dyke household staff. As when she was officially my student, I sometimes watched her try hard to meet my expectations, and fall short nonetheless.

Didrick Bent. The very name arouses such conflicting passions in me that I can't sit still. My house feels empty, but I feel as charged with electricity as the air beyond my walls.

The telephone rings on schedule. She was forbidden to contact me for two weeks, and today is the fourteenth day. I let it ring once, twice, sensing her anxiety. On the sixth ring, I answer.

"Dr. Chalkdust?" She sounds like a child. "You said I could see you today."

"Yes." She will have to express herself without help.

"I really want to come over." The tears that I would not shed are as audible in her voice as gusts of rain on glass.

"You may, Didrick," I tell her, "but you have to come here by shank's pony. Don't bring an umbrella."

"Oh, thank you," she blubbers. "I'm so—"

"Don't say it," I warn her, keeping my voice level. "What's done is done. Your apologies mean nothing, stupid girl. Be here in twenty minutes." She has a long, wet walk ahead of her, but she also has long legs with perpetual wetness between them. Even now, I suspect. The thought makes me seethe.

In due time, Didrick peers in through the glass in my oak door, her hair plastered slickly to her head like the fur of a swimming muskrat. I open the door for the tall penitent, who quickly ducks her head when she enters my hallway. I refuse to let her move past me in her dripping clothes. Her eyes drop to the floor.

"Take your clothes off and leave them here on the tiles," I tell her. I reach for a folded towel in the hall closet, and hold it as I watch her silently remove her T-shirt and denim cutoffs, then shrug out of her wet bra and pull down her underpants. Naked above the ankles, she awkwardly bends over to unlace her jogging shoes.

"Turn around to do that," I tell her.

Her face turns redder under her clinging hair. "Yes, Dr. Chalkdust," she squeaks quietly.

Presenting her firm young bottom to me, she tries to untie her shoelaces as quickly as possible, but I pull out the well-lubed butt plug I've been keeping in a plastic baggie in my pocket, and slip it into her before she has finished loosening the first shoe.

I can hear her breathing quicken, but she knows better than to protest or to pause. I twist the plug experimentally as she raises one foot to remove her shoe. I know that her movement unavoidably changes the angle of her anus in relation to the plug. I can't help smiling as she repeats the action with her other foot. The plug, shaped almost like a baby's soother, is secure by the time she must straighten up and turn to face me.

My smile is gone when I wrap the towel around her head, bent to receive it, and rub briskly as though to strike some sparks of intelligence into her brain. I run the towel down her body until there are no more droplets glistening on her skin.

Didrick's lower lip trembles. "Ah," I sigh, warning her not to lose control so soon. My warning has no effect.

She throws her strong arms around me, almost lifting me from the floor. She is openly crying, and she buries her face in the chestnut hair that flows loose over my shoulders and down my back. "I'm so sorry, Dr. C," she moans. "I never meant it to happen."

Anger flares in me. "Of course not," I answer threateningly in her ear. "You weren't prepared and you lost control. Are you going to live that way all your life, Didrick? What else do you think you might lose through sheer carelessness?"

Her tears are wetting my skin like rain, and the teasing pressure of the toy in her ass seems to be stimulating the flow from her eyes. I gently push her away. I pick up one of her competent hands, now hanging limply. "Come here," I order. "You need to see something."

I lead Didrick to the corner stand, open the glass door and pull out a white porcelain jar. "You know whose ashes are in here," I tell her. "Two weeks ago he was alive and healthy." Two photos in the stand show Pip, my blond wire-haired terrier puppy, romping in spring sunlight.

Didrick is a soggy mess. "I miss him too," she whimpers, holding the breakable jar in obvious terror of dropping it.

"Have you learned anything from that?" I ask her. "You knew he might run into the street whenever he wasn't on the leash. It was your job to protect him until he was trained."

"What can I do to make up for it?" she begs me, sniffing. I take the jar from her.

"Nothing," I explain. "But you still need to be punished for your own sake. Not for his or for mine." Her silence shows a glimmer of understanding. "To the basement," I tell her.

We descend to the permanent twilight below ground level.

I push Didrick beneath a pipe and tell her to reach up. She knows how hard this position is on the arms, even hers, if held for more than a few minutes. I find two wrist restraints on a shelf where I have left them. I climb two steps behind her, and secure her wrists to the pipe.

Without a word, I return upstairs to my kitchen, where I keep a variety of useful things. I deliberately spend some time choosing a pair of black candles, a book of matches, six clothes-pins with tight springs, a safety pin, a roll of tensor bandage and a large wooden dildo, formerly used for educational purposes in a medical school. I drop my supplies into a canvas bag and carry it to the basement.

Didrick turns as far as she can to watch my approach. I am able to slap the side of her face before I place the bandage around her eyes, cut one end and pin the ends together. Standing on a step, I reach around her to squeeze one of her small breasts, stroking the nipple until it is hard enough for my purpose. Then I snap a clothespin onto it and watch the victim flinch. I repeat the procedure with the other breast.

"How long do you think your patience will last?" I ask her. "How long do you think it took Pip to die after he had been struck by a car? He was damaged beyond repair. You aren't."

I feel almost naked without a leather belt around my waist. I remember the black one, which is still threaded through the belt-loops of a skirt in a basket of dirty laundry atop my washing machine, and I go in search of it. Pawing through my own rumpled clothes reminds me of how far the order of my house has declined in the past two weeks. Threatened by impending chaos, I am relieved to find the belt and to feel its weight as I hold it by the buckle. I want to see the changes it can effect in smooth young skin.

Didrick's anxiety is palpable in the humid room as she tries to anticipate my next move. She expects to be struck. I decide not to give her what she expects. I wrap the belt around my waist and buckle it firmly.

I return to my captive and casually run my fingernails down the damp skin stretched over her ribs. I press my head into the curve between her shoulder and her face, knowing that the scent of my hair will fill her nostrils. "You deserve punishment," I remind her softly, "but you won't get it yet. It will happen when you're not prepared. Don't you think that's appropriate, my girl?"

The bandage over her eyes is wet. "Yes, Ma'am," she whimpers. I pull the clothespins on her nipples, and this makes her squirm.

I part her legs and attach clothespins to her inner labia. I can see her thighs trembling, her solid flesh paradoxically shivering like water. I light the two candles and set them on shelves where they create brave, fragile circles of light in the dusk. I know that Didrick can see them faintly from behind her bandage.

I run both my hands down her belly to her thighs, enjoying the white tracks my fingernails leave on her tanned skin. I know that I don't have time for a leisurely exploration of her body. *Quel dommage.*

I reach up to attach my remaining two clothespins to the inner flesh of her upper arms. This is to increase her tension, and I wonder if she realizes that it also increases mine.

Didrick's cunt is giving off a distinct aroma as she shifts from one foot to the other. I want to torment her, and I want to bring her relief. I slide down her body until I am gazing into her moist, curly brown bush. I part it to find glistening pink flesh that moves slightly when I breathe on it.

She jumps when I enter her with my tongue, something I rarely do. I want the taste of her. I pull back when I can feel her hunger, and I switch to another medium. I quickly pull the clothespins off her labia, and then reach into her wet heat with two exploring fingers. I scratch her inner folds, feeling for the most sensitive spot that she can't withhold from me. I hold her open so that I can push my man Woody into her, working up a compelling rhythm. A sudden spurt and surrender inside her enables me to bury my weapon to the hilt. She moans gratefully.

I slide my fingers over her clit. She gasps loudly as the orgasm she has been trying to control seizes her in its jaws and shakes her. Her cunt clenches around its hard instructor, weeping with pleasure, as her asshole squeezes its smaller plastic bookmark. She is trembling from her stretched arms to her feet.

I wait for Didrick's last tremors to subside, and then I gently remove Woody, who looks coated in wet shellac. I climb up behind her and unfasten the wrist restraints with hands that bring her own smell closer to her nose. Her arms descend slowly, as though they had a life of their own. The movement wafts the perfume of her sweat through the air and sways the candle flames. I pull the clothespins off her arms. I release her nipples more carefully, but the rush of blood back into them makes her suck in a deep breath that shakes them.

After I have unpinned and removed the bandage from her eyes, I am pleased to see their clear light reflecting the glow of the candles. She is completely covered in a sheen of sweat, and it makes her look more heroic than I remember seeing her before: my thoughtless but loyal Amazon.

I wrap my arms around her. "One more thing, Didrick," I remind her, squeezing one of her buttocks.

"Please, Dr. Chalkdust," she answers. Her voice sounds lower and more mature than I expected.

"Please what?" I tease, reaching for the marker of my ownership still embedded in her anus.

"Please don't ever keep me away from you for this long, Ma'am." Her voice reminds me of the blues riffs of several legendary dyke singers.

I reach up to stroke her cheek. "The situation was unusual, baby," I remind her. "I don't expect it to be repeated." I hope she hears the warning as well as the assurance in my words. When I pull the plug out of her behind, she jerks in a way that feels almost rebellious, as though she were unwilling to let it go. I let her see me smile just before I blow out the candles.

In the purgatorial twilight, I reach for her hand. "Didrick," I remind her. "I'm not through with you. Come upstairs for a glass of lemonade while I consider your just deserts." The look on her face is clownish, as a grin and a look of fear struggle for dominance.

We ascend to the ground floor where sunlight streams in through my windows. The storm clouds have passed, and no trace of rain remains except the moisture on my lawn and my garden. The weather in this part of the world is as fickle as a child. Consistency must be provided by minds that can think and hearts that can feel.

I pour two glasses of lemonade and hand one to Didrick. I lead her to the sunroom. "Sit here," I tell her, gesturing toward the floor beside my peacock chair. She sinks gratefully to the hardwood and stares into the moon-yellow fluid in her glass. I notice that her nipples are still hard and red.

"I think you've grown more freckles while you've been away," I muse, "if that's possible." Her cheeks flush, and she gains the courage to glance at the mane of dark hair touched with silver that weighs damply on my neck. I gather it in both hands, lifting it away from my face. "Didrick," I order, "bring me a hair clip from the bathroom." She seems grateful to have a reason to move, or perhaps she finds my presence too unnerving.

She returns to stand beside me. "May I put it in, Dr. Chalk-dust?" she asks sweetly.

"Yes," I purr, amused. She boldly seizes my hair and her luck in both hands and deliberately lingers over her task, stroking. Her touch sends tingles through my scalp and down my spine to my neglected clit and my fasting cunt. Her strategy is as touching as it is futile. "Just fasten the clip, Didrick," I tell her. "You can brush my hair later." She reluctantly encloses my hair in its restraint as tightly as she has been taught, and withdraws from me.

"You need enough work to keep your idle hands busy," I observe. "As soon as you've finished drinking your lemonade, give all the plants a drink of water. The ones in here can't rely on rain." She hastens to obey. She must know how tempting she looks bending over the long table covered with succulents.

"You can see how much still needs to be done in this house, honey." I pet her with my gaze. Before she can guess what I require from her, I further direct her attention. "I need your eyes. Come upstairs and look down at the Persian carpet in the front room from the railing." She follows me like a puppy. I can feel her watching my asscheeks as I climb the stairs. How easily she is lured.

When I reach the second floor, I stop. "If you stand here," I explain, "you can still see the stain Pip left. Doesn't it look darker from here?"

She bends over the railing, and I hold her in place with a fist in her hair. My lips are within kissing distance of her ear. "I won't secure you, Didrick," I warn her, "but you are not allowed to move. Do you understand me?" She nods silently. I hear her swallow.

Didrick's knuckles are already white as she clutches the wooden railing. I remove my belt, grasp both ends and place myself within striking distance of the two pink cheeks that have been spared for too long. "Count them," I order just before my first stroke lands with a satisfying smack.

The second leaves a trail so red that it will become a welt within minutes. The third broadens the trail. I am not aiming with any precision because I am not aiming primarily for a visual effect. If this is careless love, it serves her well. "Five," she gasps.

"That was four," I correct her. I pause for breath. "And you're not getting the usual six this time. You're getting twelve. With one added for your mistake." My victim groans.

After the first set, I run a hand down one of her burning lower cheeks. She flinches, but maintains her position. "Good girl," I encourage her. I am tempted to test her endurance to its very limits, but that experiment can wait. I don't want to deny myself for much longer. I leave her in suspense until I see her shift her weight slightly.

I reward her with a crack of the belt that breaks the skin. The raised blood finally escapes, and I hope it releases her guilt as it cools my rage.

After the eighth stroke, I pause just long enough to catch her off guard when I deliver the ninth. A suppressed scream, flattened to a groan, slips from between her clenched teeth. Her entire buttocks are so crimson that I can't find a neglected spot. To spread my attention as fairly as possible, I aim the next at the underside of her cheeks.

"I didn't hear you," I point out. "How many?" Before she can answer, I strike again.

"Eleven," she gasps. Sometimes she justifies my faith in her capacities. The next two strokes are slightly milder. She counts each one in a barely audible voice.

I wrap my belt into a tight coil as the penitent begins to straighten up. She looks reluctant to withdraw from the railing because the muscles beneath her tender skin are reluctant to move. I catch sight of her wet face. "I'll bring you a glass of water," I promise, "and you have to drink it all."

When I return from the second-floor bathroom with a cool glass in hand, Didrick has barely moved. I can imagine her frozen in this moment for millennia, like Keats's Grecian urn. I won't allow it. "Straighten up," I command, handing her the glass while pulling her around to face me. "Stand up and breathe, baby. It's over."

I pull her against me and let her hold me. She exudes heat from every pore. "I'll tend your wounds," I promise, "after they've cooled." I kiss her and she responds by pressing her hot mouth to mine. I can taste an intoxicating mixture of anger, fear, relief and lust, with a dash of puppy love thrown in.

As she boldly slips her tongue into my mouth, I taste the strength of the woman she is becoming. I seize one of her hands and place it on one of my breasts, hoping that she can feel my heart beating underneath. "Come," I tell her. She understands me.

In my bedroom, I push her away while taking her glass from her so that I can place it and my belt atop my bureau. I pull off my T-shirt without ceremony. She confidently reaches around me to unfasten my bra, as though she were seducing a teenaged girlfriend. I wonder if she can guess that my body is undergoing a second adolescence, complete with menstrual irregularities and mysterious aches.

Enjoying the charade, I let her pull down my shorts and panties together so that her fingers graze my belly and hips. Her gentle touch is appallingly suggestive. We both know what she could do to me, and that seems to be the most forbidden topic between us.

I guide her to the bed where I slide onto the comforter and lie supine upon it, pulling her into a crouch that requires her to look down at me. Like an animal, she licks each of my nipples in turn. I wonder if she could possibly know what this means to me.

Didrick pulls my left nipple into her mouth and gradually increases the suction. My sighs seem to spur her on. "Baby," I tell her softly, "I never chose to have children." I'm not entirely sure whether I'm talking to her or to myself.

"Mm," she answers, humming around my nipple. She suddenly withdraws and looks at me. "Did you have any by accident, Ma'am?" she asks recklessly.

I can't suppress my laughter. "No, Didrick," I answer. "I was careful, as all fertile women should be." She kisses her way down my belly, either to console me for the blood-children I never had, or to remind me that I don't need them.

I am as wet and hungry and impatient as I ever was in my youth. She approaches my core, which is both altar and storm drain, with her usual impudent humility. "Do you want me, Dr. Chalkdust?" she grins.

"You brat," I laugh. "You don't deserve an answer. You know I want you. More than even I can say." I won't say that I need her.

She responds by lightly capturing my clit between her teeth as two long fingers slide into my hot darkness, the inferno that so many fools have sought out. She reaches, she discovers, she strokes. I make no effort to hide her effects on me, and I'm not quiet.

Her tongue massages my captive clit as she fills me, both of us wanting to remain so connected forever. I come with a loud gasp, clutching her fingers inside me as I clutch her head with my hands.

Quietly smug, my suitor waits for my spasms and my breathing to subside, then she slides up and tentatively lays her weight on me, using her elbows like a gentleman. I pull her head down to the space between my breasts. We breathe together.

"Oh, Didrick," I sigh. "Nothing can bring my puppy back."

I can feel her spirit sinking under leaden weights of grief, guilt and resentment. "I'm sorry, Dr. C," she mutters.

"You're not following my train of thought, baby," I chide her. "Try harder." I stroke her hair. "I still have you." I can feel the warmth of her smile.

# LUSCIOUS AND WILD

Sinclair Sexsmith

Jesse plunges three fingers into Asher's cunt, splitting her open, pushing hard past any resistance. Asher is on the tips of her toes, back arched, ass out, legs stretched long, hands and arms and cheek and even the tops of her breasts thrust against the glass of the floor-to-ceiling hotel window. She cries out. She drools and it slides down the glass, leaving a wet trail. Downtown Seattle's skyline and Puget Sound are glittering beyond the glass, the night as clear as a realism painting, and just as romantically blurred around the edges with the damp ocean air salting the city's lines.

"Oh fuck, oh my god…" Asher can't much speak. She babbles words and mostly sounds, guttural and low, come from her throat. She is being taken apart from the inside out. Jesse is sweating and so sweet on Asher she can barely stand it. Even Asher's skin is sweet: she leans in for another nibble at Asher's shoulders, and Asher gasps and leans back into her in response. Jesse reaches around her to twist and pull on her dark brown nipples, so hard and stiff after being pressed up against the cool glass.

The hotel is sleek and modern. Mostly gray, some black and white highlights dot the room. One whole wall is windows. It was a gift, this hotel weekend where they have been holed up, giggling on the pillows and fucking leisurely, with nowhere to be and nothing to do, for Asher's master's graduation and her final completion of her practicum hours. Now that the summer is over, she's even got an entry-level position at a clinic on Capitol Hill. Jesse starts her senior year of college in a few days.

But for now, there is only the two of them, luscious and wild, so eager for each other and so hungry for more.

Now that Jesse has opened up this Dominant thing, it is blooming in her like the flowers in the Arboretum after the first stripe of sun growth in March: colorful and vibrant, and made to be there.

When they first settled into the hotel, Jesse tied Asher to the bed and blindfolded her, then left her, spread-eagled, while Jesse put away their clothes and unpacked the bag of groceries they'd brought. She planned on spoiling Asher every minute of these three celebratory days and two nights. Asher kept talking, guessing, asking Jesse questions, but Jesse only answered simply: "Mm," or "Yes, I think so," or "If you ask for it, honey, you can have whatever you want."

When Jesse finally felt situated, she strapped on and slid inside Asher slowly, fucking her gently and sweetly, bodies rocking together, as Asher sucked Jesse's fingers into her mouth and Jesse touched her clit, in that soft-fast way she'd learned Asher liked, until she came.

Jesse had big plans for the scenes in this room for the weekend. And what would they do with those amazing windows? A vision started coming to Jesse as she worked out her third orgasm since the elevator.

When it was time, Jesse waited until Asher asked for it. It didn't matter how—she just had to form the words. It was what

Asher most wanted, most of the time: to be confronted with her own desire and made to look at it directly, befriend it, stop pretending like it was someone else's want that was driving the scene. It wasn't that Jesse was overpowered by lust and just had to take her, right there right now, though that was fun too—it was Asher's craving for being torn up, filled up, degraded, humiliated and used that was the impetus for most of their play. Jesse loved seeing her so filled to spilling over with her own lust that she would draw courage from some unknown well and finally start bubbling with request after request.

Maybe it's why Jesse used so much bondage—to keep Asher still and seeping in it when she finally spilled open. Being tied up is restrictive, sure, but it can also be profoundly meditative, and take someone into a safe holding where more things are possible.

Jesse loved unlocking Asher's tongue.

She had also discovered that one of Asher's most favorite things was for Jesse to get off. Maybe it's that fetish for being used, but for Jesse to lower her own cunt down over Asher's mouth, to fuck her, to jerk off over her chest or face or even right next to her cunt, and to have some spectacular orgasm, yelling and moaning, and then to leave Asher there, panting and waiting—that, that was what got Asher writhing and squirming, begging to be used again. So it was with great mutual pleasure that Jesse wracked up orgasms like points in a pinball game during their hotel weekend. She kept track, telling Asher aloud how many times it had been.

In Asher's ear at the hotel window, Jesse whispers, "Seven, Asher. I'm all the way up at seven, and how many times have you come?"

Asher whimpers. Her clit is hard and swollen, her lips puffy and thick. Her mouth is red from sucking.

"How many?"

"Once," Asher whispers.

"That's right, once. And you weren't really supposed to be coming, were you? You just couldn't help it?"

"I couldn't help it! You made me do it, I...I'm sorry, I didn't mean to. I like following your rules, I just...it was too much. I couldn't help it!" She thrums the words in that husky low tone she gets when she is so turned on.

"Shh, it's okay, baby. I know. It was my fault, I don't expect to fuck you that much and not have you come...at least some-times." Jesse laughs a little to herself, thrilled and giddy. She strokes Asher's cunt, every contour, every swollen slick place. She gets juicy enough as it is, but Jesse still adds more lube, more wetness. She traces lines with the pads of her fingers and uses them to pinch and apply pressure, catching the head of Asher's clit between them, palming her whole vulva, pinching her lips together, which makes Asher squirm and shiver.

Jesse slides her fingers in again, in and out, stopping in all the spots that she knows Asher likes. "How many times are you going to come for me now, if I let you?"

"How many...times? Two. Three. Five. How many do you want me to come?" Asher's words aren't quite making sense, but she thrusts her hips back toward Jesse and presses her chest and cheek into the glass, offering herself up, willing Jesse not to stop.

"Five, huh? That's a lot. Could you come on demand, if I just tell you to come right now, could you do it?"

"Could I come...right now? I don't...really know." Asher puzzles a little, gets distracted by Jesse's fingers, then starts thinking again, trying to figure out how much her mind has control over her body. "Maybe? I think so. Yeah, actually. Tell me to do it! Jesse, tell me, and I'll do it, I'll do it for you, when-ever you say."

"Really? You think you could?" Still, in and out, slowly, with Jesse's thumb circling Asher's clit.

"Yes! Oh yes, I'll show you, I can do it for you."

"Okay, baby, ready? Come...right now."

"Ohhhhhh," Asher cries out, her cunt pulsing hard, pushing and contracting and pushing until she gushes onto Jesse's hand.

"That's one. Can you do it again for me? Can I keep going?"

"Yes, yes keep going, don't stop don't stop…"

"You're so fucking hot, Ash. I love watching you like this. Come again girl, do it, let's have it all. Now!"

"Fuck, fuckfuckfuck!" Asher yells, arms sliding down the glass as if she can't hold them up any longer. Her knees and thighs shake. Jesse pushes her hand farther inside and Asher gasps, pushing her hips open.

"Two," Jesse growls in her ear. "Keep going. Ready to do it again for me, slut? Didn't get all you needed yet, huh? Can you do it again?"

"Yes, yes yes yesssss," Asher moans, wetness dripping down Jesse's hand and wrist.

"Three." Jesse is practically giggling now, high and strong, and she could do this for hours: keep Asher poised on her fingers, begging and coming.

"Four! Please four, Jesse, please, four—" Asher begs. She squirms and tries to close her legs, trying to back off from the orgasms that still want to claim her cunt.

"Now. Do it," comes Jesse's reply, low and growly at Asher's neck. Jesse bites at her earlobe and Asher throws her head back to rest on Jesse's shoulder, sighing, breathing, still moaning those sounds from her throat.

"One more," Jesse reminds her. "One more, and then we're all done. Can you do it again?"

"Nooo, no Jesse, I don't think I can, I don't know…it's too much, I can't."

"You can do it. Remember how you told me five? Actually, you said, 'How many do you want me to come,' but I want five. So five it is. That's one more." Jesse makes the gentlest circles over Asher's swollen cunt, soft and fast on her clit, that way that she likes.

"I can't, I can't, Jesse...oh god, oh my god, oh my fuck fuuuuck..." Asher trails off and comes again, legs shaking, body humming, throat humming, practically sliding all the way down the window to the floor if it wasn't for Jesse's leg in between hers. Jesse holds her up for a moment, then lets them both collapse down, catching Asher in her arms and wrapping around her naked body as she shivers and settles.

"I can't believe you made me! You. You! Are incredible. I love you." Asher nuzzles into Jesse's shoulder, and Jesse braces herself against the bed to hold them both upright. They laugh and talk and stroke each other, doing that postfucking, hazy, loopy thing where everything is hilarious and important.

Eventually, Jesse says, "My foot's asleep. And also, want some food?"

Asher lights up. "I'm starved. I feel like I have never eaten before ever. I want all the things!"

Jesse starts untangling, and moves to stand. "Oh that's good, because we bought all the things at the grocery store before we came. I'm hungry too. C'mon, let's get up. You okay to stand?"

"Yeah. Okay." Asher reaches up for Jesse's arms and accepts help to get steady on her feet.

# SMORGASBORD

R. G. Emanuelle

Renee surveyed the smorgasbord on her dining room table. Truffles, spreads and pestos of various colors, and buttery vegetables were laid out within reach.

She stuck a finger in the hummus and scooped some out. With the very tip of her tongue, she tasted it, then flung it onto the canvas. She regarded the splatters for a moment, then scooped up a handful of steamed baby peas and dropped them, one by one, over the pesto.

She stepped back and stared at the canvas. No, this wasn't right. She rubbed her forehead, hoping to dispel both the headache and frustration of the past two weeks, filled with fits and starts on this project.

Renee sighed and decided that she needed a break. She'd go to the art show she'd been invited to. Quickly, she threw on something clean and presentable and left her project in the dark.

Renee walked around the gallery, briefly studying each piece displayed on the walls. She was more captivated by the bold

Malbec in her hand and the Manchego at the cocktail station.

After an hour, she began looking for a way to escape unobtrusively. But there was only one exit, and the artist was squarely in front of it.

A thick blanket of pretentiousness in the room was smothering her and she decided to step outside for air. The gallery's garden was flanked on two sides by large oak trees, and stone benches dotted the perimeter. Chinese lanterns illuminated the area with a soft light.

The garden was usually a popular place for people who needed air or a smoke, but tonight there were only three others, and when Renee walked out, two of them went back inside the gallery.

A lone woman sat on a bench, sipping a glass of red and staring at a vine of climbing roses. Her hair was set in two braids of black with streaks of blood red through them, echoing the wine in her hand. The movement of her breathing made her glass sparkle with refracted light.

What to say to such a beautiful woman? Maybe she was hungry. A good woman never refused food.

Renee dashed back inside and moved quickly through the crowds of art lovers until she spotted a server holding a tray. The server smiled and lowered the tray. "Mushroom *en croute?*"

"Yes, please." Renee took a napkin, picked up two of the little dumplings, and returned to the garden. Back outside, she took a deep breath and walked over to the woman. She was now looking at a stone fountain sculpted into a female figure in flowing robes, emptying a bucket into a pool.

Renee approached her cautiously, not wanting to startle her, but did anyway. The woman jumped a little as she turned. "Oh!"

"I'm sorry," Renee said, feeling a bit startled herself. "You looked like you could use a little something." She held out the napkin with the mushroom *en croute,* slightly smashed. She hadn't realized that she'd squeezed them. "Oh," she said, embarrassed. "I'm really sorry. These were good-looking a minute ago."

The woman chuckled. "It still looks good, just a little more... rustic."

Renee's heart skipped a beat. It wasn't often she met a woman at these functions who had a genuine sense of humor.

"Thank you." The woman took one of the hors d'oeuvres and shoved the entire thing in her mouth, then daintily whisked away the flaky crumbs around her lips. Not what Renee was expecting, but cute.

"Well, how is it?" she asked.

"Not bad. Try it."

Renee popped the other one into her mouth. "Mmm."

"I'm Delilah." The woman put her hand out.

Delilah? How poetic.

"Renee." She shook Delilah's hand.

"Do you want to sit?" Delilah scooted over.

Renee sat, suddenly aware that she had lost her Malbec. She motioned a server who was going around with Bellinis. When she'd gotten one, she asked, "So, what do you do?"

"I'm a writer."

"Are you covering the installation?"

"No. My coworker scored me an invitation. I have a food column in the *Tribune*."

Renee turned toward her. "The *Tribune*? You're Delilah Ramsey? I read your column all the time."

Delilah blushed. "Thanks." She scanned Renee's hands and arms, crossed loosely against her chest, and stopped at her face. Renee could feel each part turning red, as if Delilah were searing her skin with her gaze.

Renee gripped the carved stone beneath her to keep from sliding off. Delilah's green eyes were deep and multilayered, with hints of wisdom, like she'd lived twenty lives.

"Are you a foodie?" Delilah asked.

"I suppose." Renee chuckled. "I work with food."

"Really? Are you a chef?"

"No."

"Then how so?"

"I use food as part of my art."

Delilah's eyes narrowed a bit and her voice lowered when she said, "I'd love to see some of your work."

Renee swallowed. "Um, sure. I'd love to show you."

Delilah regarded her a moment and Renee felt herself flare with heat. "You looked as bored as I was when you walked out here. How's about we go now?"

"Now?" Renee suddenly felt ill.

Delilah peered around Renee to look through the glass doors and into the gallery. Inside, artists were chatting with patrons and reporters, flutes of champagne in their hands, everyone dressed in customary black. "Yes. Let's blow this Popsicle stand."

Renee's apartment was sparsely furnished, the space taken up by canvases, sculptures and artists' paraphernalia.

"Wow, this must get a lot of light," Delilah said.

"Yeah, that's what I love about this place. The natural light is great. But, as you can see, it's small. I need to move."

"I know what you mean. I need an entire room for all my cooking equipment."

Renee slung her jacket over a chair. "Would you like some coffee? A drink?"

"Coffee would be great."

She went into the kitchen, separated from the rest of the apartment by a bar-style counter.

While the coffee dripped, Delilah walked around the loft, pausing at different pieces of art to study them. She stopped at a framed painting of a beachscape in which orange slices splayed across the horizon. "This is fantastic. You're very creative."

"So are you. Those recipes you come up with always sound so delicious."

"But you take food to a whole new level." She admired it for another moment. "How do you keep the food from rotting? Do you spray something on it?"

"Yes. It's a special varnish. A couple of coats, and food is preserved indefinitely."

"Like a bug in amber."

Renee laughed. "Yeah, I suppose."

Renee poured two mugs of coffee and placed them on the counter. "Half-and-half okay?"

"Absolutely. I don't understand skim milk in coffee." Delilah walked over to the counter and sat on one of the stools. She frowned. "Makes it look and taste like dirty bathwater."

Renee's chest fluttered. A foodie, a sense of humor and wry. *Now, if only she's into music, she'd be my dream woman.* "Do you like music?"

"Love it. What do you like?"

"A little of everything. Rock, dance, jazz, blues, alternative."

"Me, too! My favorite, though, is slow and soulful. Like Joss Stone."

*She's Venus. I've just met Venus.* "I think I have some cookies somewhere."

"No, thanks. You're sweet enough."

Renee's ears rang as blood rushed to her head. Was she still in an upright position?

"So, tell me about what's going on over there." Delilah pointed her chin in the direction of the table with the canvas lying on it.

"I'm working on a project. After the positive reactions I got on my last installation, *Culinary Adventures* magazine wants me to do a photo project. But it's not working. I keep trying different things, but it's just not happening."

"Why are you having such a hard time?"

"I don't know. Something's missing."

"Well, what exactly are you doing?"

"I'm preparing certain foods and using them as the paint on the canvas."

She looked over at the table. "What kind of foods?"

"For this one, chocolate—in truffle and ganache forms—fava bean spread, cherries, cilantro pesto..." Renee started to feel foolish. Delilah must think she was nuts.

"That sounds sexy."

"That's good. I was going for sexy."

"Well, I'm not that experienced with art, but I'd be happy to brainstorm with you...if that would help."

Renee wasn't sure how to respond. On the one hand: beautiful woman, willing to spend time with her and discuss her work. On the other hand: total stranger.

"I'd love that. Maybe we can have dinner sometime?" Renee tried to look casual by sipping her coffee.

"How about this Friday?"

Renee's throat went dry. She took another swig. Hot coffee, she discovered, does nothing to help moisten a parched throat. "I'd love to."

"Great." Delilah smiled, and then looked at her watch. "I have to go. I have a dinner date at nine." She slid off the stool.

"Okay," Renee said, trying not to sound disappointed. "Um, I should give you my number."

"No need. I'll pick you up Friday at seven, okay?"

She tried to control her smile so that it didn't turn into a dumb-ass grin. "Sounds intriguing. I'm looking forward to it."

"Me, too." Delilah pulled her jacket on and picked up her purse. "Thanks for the coffee."

"Anytime," Renee replied, as Delilah walked out her door.

Renee must have pulled out every pair of pants, shirt and skirt and tried them on with every pair of shoes. She had to hurry, though—she had just buzzed Delilah up.

She had no idea where Delilah was taking her. A fancy place? Casual? Pizza? She finally decided on something neutral—a pair of gray slacks and a royal-blue button-down blouse. She was fastening a simple chain-link silver necklace when the doorbell rang. Her hands began trembling and she lost her grip on the clasp. The doorbell rang again.

"Damn!" She ran out with the chain in her hand and stopped at the door for a second to regain her composure, then opened it.

Delilah stood there wearing black jeans and motorcycle boots and a black pullover with a collared white shirt. Okay, casual.

"Hi," Renee said.

"Hi. You ready?"

"Sure. Let me just grab my jacket. Come in for a sec."

While Delilah waited by the door, Renee attempted once more to get the chain around her neck. She struggled for a minute before Delilah came over. "Here, let me help you." She took the chain and brought it around Renee's throat. Renee felt her fingers on the nape of her neck and shivered, hoping that it wasn't obvious. When Delilah had clasped the chain, her fingers remained on Renee's skin—only for a second or two, but enough to make Renee's belly tighten.

"Thanks." Renee put her jacket on. "Okay, let's go."

Despite her angst, the car ride was comfortable, and before long, Delilah pulled up at a curb.

"Here we are."

Renee looked out the window. They had parked in front of a row of brick houses. She didn't see a restaurant. "Here?"

"Yeah." Delilah got out of the car and went up on the sidewalk, where she waited for her. Renee followed.

"Um, where's the restaurant?"

"This way." Delilah led her up the block a couple of yards and turned in toward a pinkish brick house with an iron fence enclosing a little shrub garden. She led Renee up the driveway to a side door, and up a flight of stairs.

Delilah kept silent until they reached the top and walked into a vestibule. From there, they entered a dining room.

A rectangular, rough-hewn wooden table was prepared with two place settings, wineglasses and candles. A round, squat vase filled with white chrysanthemums sat in the center.

"Oh, wow," Renee said, "What is this?"

"This is the restaurant. It's called Delilah's Kitchen," she said with a playful grin.

Renee was stunned. "I don't know what to say."

"Well, don't just stand in the doorway. Come in."

Renee walked cautiously toward the table, afraid to disturb anything.

On the table was a platter of what looked like artichoke hearts and a bottle of chenin blanc. "I feel terrible. I didn't bring anything. Why didn't you tell me? I would've brought wine or dessert or—"

"Everything tonight is on me, including the wine and dessert."

Renee stood motionless. A strange sensation rippled through her, like a combination of settling into a warm blanket on a cold wintry day and sticking your finger in a light socket. She went to the entrance of the kitchen. Equipment filled almost every inch of space. "That is the biggest food processor I've ever seen in my life," she said.

"I bet you say that to all the girls."

"Actually, I don't," Renee responded with a snort.

Delilah nodded. "Yeah, I kind of have a weakness for kitchen toys. I do so much cooking, it pays to have the good stuff." She shrugged. "Why don't you open up the wine? I'll finish up in here."

Renee went back to the table, picked up the corkscrew and began working on the bottle. "Well, not too soon, I hope." Her voice caught slightly.

Delilah joined her and bent over to pick up the two wine-glasses. "Do you have somewhere to be after dinner?"

"No."

"Then we've got all night."

Renee's hand trembled slightly as she poured the wine.

"Let's go sit in the living room while the food finishes cooking."

They sat on her couch, an intimate thing that would have held three people at most. "Here's to new friends." Delilah held up her glass.

"To new friends." Renee clinked her glass against Delilah's and sipped. She needed the fortification.

Over the wine, they chatted about Renee's work and her methods until a rich, savory aroma began to waft in.

"Something smells amazing. What is that?"

"Swedish meatballs."

Renee looked at her sideways. "You are a goddess."

Delilah laughed. "Hardly. It's not as complicated as people think. At least, my version isn't."

In the moment of silence that followed, and under Delilah's gaze, Renee felt as if nothing else in the world existed. There was only here and now.

The spell was broken when Delilah got up. "I think they're ready."

Renee followed her out. "Can I help?"

"Absolutely not. Have a seat at the table."

"I feel funny not doing anything. I mean, you cooked dinner—"

"I've got it under control."

Renee sat down at the table. Two bamboo placemats held white square plates and cloth napkins folded inside wooden napkin rings. "You set a beautiful table," she called out to the kitchen.

"Thank you," Delilah responded, as she brought in a small

platter. She set it on the table and sat down. "Please, help your-self."

Renee picked up two of the little meatballs by the toothpicks sticking out of them and put them in her plate. Delilah then picked up the artichokes. "Try these."

"They look great." She took a spoonful of the hearts and tasted raspberry vinaigrette.

Dinner conversation was light and comfortable as they made their way through Delilah's menu: trofie with pesto, blackened catfish with red quinoa, and sauteed bok choy.

"You know," Delilah said, after they'd eaten everything on their plates. "I'd like to do a story on you. An artist who uses food in her art. Not just in the usual way, like crushing berries for paint, but actually using food in the art."

"Um, okay."

"I hope you left room for dessert. I made it fresh."

"You *made* dessert, too?"

"Of course." She batted her eyes coquettishly. "Why don't you go into the living room? I'll bring dessert in there."

Within a couple of minutes, Delilah entered with two sundae glasses in her hands. "Chocolate Kahlúa pudding."

Renee's jaw dropped. "Oh. My. God. You can't be serious."

Delilah placed them on the coffee table. "You seem to have a predilection for chocolate."

They both scooped spoonfuls into their mouths. Renee closed her eyes and moaned. "This is incredible," she murmured.

Delilah smiled. "It's one of my signature dishes. I've made it a thousand times. Funny, I was worried it wouldn't come out right."

"Why?"

Delilah blushed and Renee melted.

"I really wanted it to come out good for you."

The pudding was soft and warm and it made her think of Delilah's flesh, her shoulders, breasts, and possibly touching all of them with her lips. She quickly stuck another spoonful in her mouth.

"I love chocolate, too," Delilah continued. "There's something so sensual about it. It's smooth, silky, rich and complex. And, of course, chocolate triggers endorphins. It's a known aphrodisiac."

Renee swallowed. "Does that mean you're trying to seduce me?"

They stared at each other for a long moment. Renee looked at Delilah's braids, following the path of one red streak, weaving in and out of the ropes of hair, winding like a river. Then, both began nervously laughing. Delilah dribbled pudding onto her shirt and wiped it, still laughing.

"Uh-oh, I hope that comes out."

"It's okay, I'm used to spilling food on myself."

Renee watched her calmly dab her shirt with her napkin, and it dawned on her. The thing her project was missing.

"Would you be willing to help me with my project?"

Delilah's eyes widened. "I'd love to! What do you need me to do?"

Renee told her what she had in mind. Although Delilah seemed hesitant at first, she agreed.

Despite the incredible dinner she'd just had, Renee felt ill again. Thinking about what she was going to do with Delilah was almost too much to think about.

Three days later, Delilah sat at Renee's counter in a robe with her laptop and began her story while Renee prepared her workspace.

Renee draped a drop cloth over the dining room table and smoothed it out. "Okay, lie down." Delilah untied the robe and slowly let it drop off her shoulders and slide down her body. Renee swallowed hard. Delilah was stunning, from the curve of her plump breasts to her smooth thighs. For a second, she wondered what it would be like to lay her head down on those breasts after a long, hard day. Her full thighs and curvaceous hips would make a sumptuous canvas.

Delilah lay down, her hair settled gently around her head. Renee's head grew hot. She tried not to appear as if she was interested in Delilah's body but didn't know how to do that. She *had* to look at her, so she furrowed her brow and tried to look pensive.

She stood near Delilah's face. "Are you okay?"

Delilah, hands folded on her stomach and feet crossed, wiggled her toes anxiously. "Yes. I'm a little nervous. It's not every day that I'm part of someone's art. A *naked* part of someone's art." She gave Renee a small smile, which she took to mean that Delilah was still willing.

"So, I'm going to take the various foods and place them on different parts of your body. Ready?"

Delilah nodded and stoically put her hands to her side. "Ready."

Renee turned to the bowls and plates of food on the card table she'd set up next to the dining table and picked up the first bowl, containing macerated blackberries. She scooped some out and looked Delilah over. With a paintbrush, she made a circle on her stomach with vertical lines stemming out above and below the circle. To that, she added a splash of crimson from the bowl of red-pepper puree.

One by one, she took each food and determined where it should be on Delilah's body.

The ripe white figs went perfectly between her breasts, and the honey dripping down along her rib cage made Delilah's nipples harden, making Renee shiver. The caramel, still warm, awakened her skin with gooseflesh as Renee drizzled it back and forth all along her torso, making her look like a pastry.

The air became redolent of basil and cinnamon from infused chocolate ganache, which Renee spread on her lower belly.

"Oh, that smells so good," Delilah said, sniffing the air.

"I try to engage all the senses." She ran her fingers over Delilah's skin, pulling champagne slurry along. Delilah shivered.

"Are you cold?"

Delilah's cheeks flushed rosy. "No."

When she'd blanketed Delilah from head to toe with the sumptuous feast, Renee picked up her camera and said, "You are a smorgasbord."

Delilah smiled shyly. Then Renee began shooting. It was difficult keeping her eye in the viewfinder and not on the shimmering pomegranate seeds or peaches, glistening with their own cooked sugars, sliding in tiny increments across Delilah's skin.

She shot from all sides and from above, individual body parts as well as the whole. Many shots later, she put the camera down.

"Well, that's it, I think. You must be stiff."

"A little." Delilah brought her knees up, making berry juice run down her thighs.

"I'll get some towels." Renee looked at the figs between Delilah's breasts. "What a shame to waste all this perfectly good food," she said with a chuckle.

"We don't have to waste it."

Renee's heart pounded. Was that an invitation? She reached for a fig, then pulled her hand back. Cautiously, she bent over and picked one up with her mouth. When her lips met Delilah's flesh, Delilah's stomach tightened. Renee felt as liquid as the nectar on Delilah's belly. With the fig still between her lips, she moved up to Delilah's face and touched the fig to her lips.

Delilah gently bit and gazed up at Renee, who bent again and kissed her. Delilah encouraged her with a hand. She loosened herself from Delilah's grip and pulled off her T-shirt and bra. She climbed on top of the table and lowered herself slowly onto Delilah, one leg between hers.

She licked caramel off her stomach, nibbled mango from her arms and sucked the raspberry coulis that had settled on

Delilah's fingers. Her shoulders, dusted in toasted coconut, were next, then the hollow of her throat, which cupped slivered almonds and pooled balsamic reduction. She kissed the taste of lavender on her neck.

Delilah writhed and arched beneath Renee's lips. The aroma of sweet sugars and fragrant herbs mingled with the scent of need.

Delilah tugged at Renee's pants and Renee obliged by removing them and her underwear and tossing them aside. She repositioned herself on Delilah and continued tasting the menu. She slowly slid her hand down her torso until she reached her thighs and slipped her fingers between them. Delilah gasped.

She swirled a finger in the caramel and pulled some down where she could taste it and Delilah at the same time. One lick made Delilah moan. Renee continued licking, stopping now and then to add something else from the smorgasbord, as if they were condiments for Delilah's body. Renee had her tongue deep inside. Delilah tasted like ambrosia, and she knew that it wasn't the sweets.

Delilah's breathing was hard and ragged and she gripped Renee's shoulders. Renee, with her arms wrapped around her thighs, flattened her hands against Delilah's belly, smashing avocado and hazelnut-espresso mousse together in her fingers. Slippery, thick and sticky, it echoed what was coating Renee's tongue. The sweet, salty, umami taste of Delilah intoxicated her even more as Delilah came on her tongue.

Delilah sat up, any semblance of design in the food completely eradicated. Colors and flavors were spread and combined all over her torso and limbs. She gently forced Renee into a sitting position and then straddled her so that they faced each other and their legs were intertwined. From her own torso, she gathered a combination of fruits and honey on her fingertip, and fed Renee the sweet mélange.

Renee bit gently down on Delilah's finger, startling her. But she didn't pull away. Instead, she pushed her finger in more, letting Renee stroke it with her lips. Delilah finally pulled her finger away and picked up a small paintbrush that Renee had left at her side and dipped it on herself, as if she were a palette of paints. A little red, a little blue, a little orange, she painted each of Renee's nipples with this mixture.

Renee closed her eyes and tilted her head up, savoring the delicious sensation. Then, Delilah's lips were on her neck, nibbling, and every nerve ending sparked, every part of her ached for release, like a pressure cooker left too long on the heat.

Delilah brought her hand down between Renee's legs where she was so wet that the hand sank right in. Delilah kissed her as she stroked, and Renee became dizzy. She was shocked by a searing sensation on her clit, and she came hard.

Renee pushed herself up. Delilah's face was flushed and her eyes still glazed with her own orgasm. Her lips were bright red and Renee kissed her. She looked Delilah over. "I think you could use a shower."

"Think so?"

"Yes. Let me help you with that."

They both slid off the table and went to the bathroom.

After they'd showered, Delilah helped Renee clean up the dining room.

"We probably should've done this before showering," Delilah said.

Renee laughed. "Uh, yeah."

"Wanna grab something to eat?" Delilah asked.

"You're hungry?"

"I'm always hungry." Her voice and eyes told Renee that she wasn't just talking about food.

If life was a dish, soul was the inspiration, passion the recipe and love the seasoning. The ingredients make it all worthwhile.

"Let's go," Renee said as she handed Delilah her jacket.

Delilah pulled her into another deep, long kiss.

"Planning any more projects?"

"Mmm, maybe," Delilah said with a grin. "Come on. I want to take you somewhere really special." And as they walked down the stairs, she took Renee's hand. "Did I mention that I really love food?"

# A PROFESSIONAL

Rose P. Lethe

"I don't usually get female clients." Mei kept her tone light, not letting on how grave an understatement it was.

She *never* got female clients, nor did any other pro Domme she had ever met. Aside from the rare heterosexual couple (often a cautious but devoted woman seeking to please her male partner, but more common lately was a man looking for advice on how to satisfy his female partner's bondage fantasies), it was all men: men wanting to submit, men wanting to be hurt, men wanting to indulge an obscure or embarrassing fetish. Women, straight or otherwise, who were looking for the same went elsewhere.

Which was why Mei had been so interested in meeting the one woman in the entire city who was seeking a one-on-one session with a professional Domme.

The woman didn't disappoint. Dark-haired, green-eyed and light-skinned, probably in her midthirties like Mei, sitting primly on the other side of the circular table, Jennifer Carnes popped the lid off her cup of coffee and curled her red-painted lips into a smirk. A full face of makeup, long brown hair neatly curled and arranged artfully over her shoulders, and she even smelled faintly of perfume and hairspray—she was so femme she probably got mistaken for straight daily, but she wasn't. Mei's instincts were never wrong about that sort of thing.

"You mean you *never* get female clients," Jennifer said. "The other women I contacted were more blunt about it."

Impressed, Mei sat back in her chair, which creaked and wobbled. This was her favorite coffeehouse for meeting new clients—she loved the coffee and the privacy the unusually wide spaces between tables allowed her—but she could also admit that it was in poor shape. "So I'm not the first Domme you called?"

Jennifer shrugged. "Of course not. You're just the only one who didn't immediately turn me down."

That was a bit surprising, although Mei didn't see any point in dwelling on what other people did or didn't do. She mimicked Jennifer's shrug and tidied her papers. "Well. You've seen my website, obviously, so you know what I offer. You said on the phone that you were interested in pain."

Jennifer took a sip of coffee, leaving behind a bright red lip print on the cup's rim. "Just pain. None of the submissiveness or role-playing, definitely no pretense of punishment. I like it sharp and stingy. Knife play is my favorite, actually."

"No blood," Mei said sharply. "No bodily fluids of any kind."

Jennifer smiled. There was an edge to it that made Mei suspect she was being silently laughed at, which was…interesting. This meeting really wasn't what she had expected at all. "I know," said Jennifer. "I saw your website, remember? That was just an example, so you know the sort of pain I like."

She took another, longer drink of coffee. When she'd swallowed, she pressed her lips together in something that was reminiscent of, but much more dignified than, a smack. She had the air of a former Catholic schoolgirl, Mei thought. Like she'd tried to shuck good manners and ladylike behavior but found them too deeply ingrained.

"Anyway." Jennifer replaced the lid and scooted the cup away from her. "I was thinking a little spanking to start with. Bent over something, preferably. I *hate* standing or lying down. Then a good thrashing with a riding crop once I'm warmed up. Make sure you leave marks. I love marks."

Mei couldn't help but arch an eyebrow. She was becoming even more impressed as the meeting went on. "That's very specific."

"Mm-hm." Yes, Jennifer was definitely laughing at her. There was an amused little gleam in her eyes. "Well, I know what I want. What are those?" She gestured toward the papers in Mei's hands.

"Forms." Mei handed them over. "There's a questionnaire about your limits and preferences, an information sheet about your general health and a waiver. Take them with you; read them carefully, especially the last one. Make sure you fill everything out completely. I'll review them and discuss any concerns I have with you before our first session. Assuming you're still interested."

"I am." Jennifer's voice was faraway, distracted, while she flipped from page to page. Eventually, she set the whole stack aside, balancing it on the lid of her coffee. "I'm still interested. Same rate you mentioned on the phone?"

Mei nodded and held Jennifer's gaze, waiting for any further questions. There were always questions during her first meetings with her clients: about safety, privacy, accepted forms of payment. All of it was already answered on her website, but people still liked to ask.

Jennifer, though, only stared back. She'd have made a decent Domme herself, Mei thought. Or at least, she had the attitude for it: the vaguely mocking demeanor, the self-assurance, the matter-of-factness.

"Is that all?" Jennifer asked, pulling Mei from her thoughts.

"If you don't have any other questions." Mei's own drink, a caramel macchiato, had been largely untouched until now, so she dragged it closer and took a drink. It was cool, but not undrinkable.

"No, I don't." Jennifer cocked her head, catlike. "Do *you*?"

Oh yes, Mei decided, she liked this one. A confident, upfront woman who would be fun to bend over her lap and spank until she was bruised and squirming.

*Don't get carried away*, Mei reminded herself. *She's a client.*

Aloud, she said, "Why are you looking for a professional, if you don't mind me asking? The city's got an active kink community. There are lots of dominant women who'd be happy to hurt you for free."

Jennifer wilted. Not greatly, more like a hanging picture beginning to dip on one side, but enough that Mei understood immediately she'd overstepped. Before she could take it back, however, Jennifer drew herself up again, a little nudge to rebalance the crooked frame, and answered.

"Sure. But most of the ones I've met are poly." One shoulder rose and fell. "And apparently I'm not. I keep...getting too attached." Jennifer scooped up the stack of papers and turned around to stuff them in the handbag hanging on the back of her chair. "Anyway. If that's all, then I'll be off. Thank you for meeting me. I'll be in touch, erm...Mistress Cheng?"

It sounded wrong in Jennifer's voice: not just the hesitation and the questioning lilt, but the title itself. She was asking for pain, after all, not submission, so Mei didn't even think before she said, "Just call me Mei."

The sessions were never sexual for Mei.

Not because she didn't have any interest in domination and sadism (that was how she'd gotten into pro Domming in the first place, after all), but because her clients were men. And whatever those men thought of her, Mei didn't and had never thought sexually about them.

She dominated men; she fucked women.

She used to fuck women, anyway. It had been years since Mei had met anyone who wasn't put off by her profession. Understandable, she supposed—understandable but lonely.

It didn't occur to her until she was looking over Jennifer's paperwork before their session that she was about to cross a rather significant boundary in her work.

"I must say," Jennifer said, skimming her fingers along the top of the burgundy velvet chaise lounge that Mei had hauled from one of the other rooms just this morning, "your dungeon's not what I expected." She was dressed differently than she had been during their first meeting. Her makeup, if she was wearing any, was minimal, her hair was gathered into a high ponytail, and she wore jeans and a gray hoodie. It made her look at least a decade younger. "More...homey."

Of course it was. It was a house, after all. Mei shrugged, turning a page to peruse Jennifer's questionnaire. "I rent it with three other Dommes. The basement setup is probably more in line with what you were imagining, but I thought you'd prefer this."

"You were right. I also appreciate that you're not wearing, you know, seven-inch heels and a corset."

Mei had predicted that as well, and dressed more androgynously than she might've with another client: a black suit and black shoes, her shoulder-length hair swept into a low ponytail. She hadn't bothered with makeup; she would only sweat it off.

Jennifer fingered the zipper of her hoodie. "Should I go ahead and undress?"

"Sure." Mei rose from the chaise, setting the papers aside to be filed later. "I noticed you put down a strong interest in rope bondage." Hair pulling and scratching were also listed, but those were more in line with Mei's expectations and not worth asking about.

"For future sessions." Jennifer's voice was muffled. Mei glanced over to find her tugging a red fitted T-shirt over her head, exposing a satiny black bra. "Today I just want the pain, like I said. Will the bondage cost extra?"

How very, very different she was from Mei's other clients. Most masochists wanted at least a hint of submission, or expressed some hesitation about making overt demands. Which was stupid, obviously, since they were the paying customers, but that was how it was. Mei didn't bother stifling her amusement when she answered, "No, the cost is the same."

She watched as Jennifer finished undressing. She unhooked her bra and then removed her jeans, followed by her black cotton hip-hugging panties. Her movements were leisurely and graceful; if she was self-conscious about standing nude in front of a stranger, she hid it well.

Not that she had anything to be self-conscious about—Mei had seen it all, as far as human bodies were concerned, and Jennifer's was lovely. Her hips were wide, her thighs thick and her breasts full and heavy, hanging in a way that suggested she'd gained and lost a significant amount of weight. Her belly looked soft but not round, and it was striped with faded stretch marks on either side of her navel that reminded Mei of claw marks.

Her pubic hair was long and unkempt: a poof of wiry curls blooming from where the tops of her thighs met. Her skin seemed paler than it had previously: almost translucent, her veins a muted blue beneath it. There was a brownish bruise on Jennifer's left knee, a violet-blue one on her left bicep.

She would bruise beautifully, artistically. Mei could see it now: the bleed of colors on her skin like paints on a canvas.

Mei came closer, circling around the back of the chaise just as Jennifer draped herself on her stomach across it, sprawling for a moment like a house cat before rising to her knees and bending over the arm, with her bottom turned up perfectly to be smacked. Her ass was plump, the cheeks dimpled slightly like ripples in a pond.

Oh yes, this was very different from Mei's male clients.

But she wouldn't let it show. She would behave as she always did.

As Mei approached the chaise, she trailed her fingertips up the length of Jennifer's spine. The touch made Jennifer's muscles jerk and her body heave forward. She turned her head to the side, resting her right cheek on her folded arms and gazing at Mei through half-lidded eyes. Mei paid little attention to her expression, too intent on exploring the hills and valleys of her back.

She kept her touch gentle and reassuring, working to slow Jennifer's thoughts to a lull. Mei had met dozens of masochists over the years, with an eclectic range of experiences and psychologies, and she would bet anything that Jennifer was one of the ones for whom the pain was incidental—what she craved most was someone to help her out of her own head.

Mei's hand traced her left scapula and followed the fading wrinkle from her bra strap to her shoulder and then down her arm. Jennifer had an assortment of tiny marks on her hands and wrists, ranging from puffy and red to smooth and pink.

"What are these?"

Jennifer blinked, her brows drawing together. "Burns. From a curling iron, mostly. I work as a hairdresser. Common hazard of the trade."

A hairdresser. Mei pictured her sweeping hair off the floor, the bruises and welts on her ass aching with every step.

Humming in acknowledgment, Mei skimmed her fingers through the hair spilling from Jennifer's ponytail. The strands were soft, shiny, well cared for. Jennifer made a murmured noise of pleasure and dropped her head forward so that Mei could stroke the tufts of hair at her nape.

"Safewords?"

"Yellow to slow down." Jennifer wriggled her bottom playfully, as though reminding Mei to get on with it. "Red to stop."

"Mm-hm." Mei retracted her hand and stepped back. "We'll start with spanking, then move to the crop. Unless you've changed your mind? I've got a nice range of floggers, including a little rubber one that's—"

"No." It was an impatient-sounding scoff. In most cases, it might've tempted Mei to issue a sharp slap to the face—although whether she'd have followed through would've depended on the client's preferences and limits—but now it only made her snort, amused. "Just the spanking and the crop."

Fair enough, Mei supposed. She took her position, standing an arm's length away and laying her right hand flat in the center of Jennifer's plump ass: memorizing the position, picturing the arc her hand would take, calculating the amount of force required. Then she raised her arm and swung.

She kept the blow light—this was a warm-up, after all—but with her palm slightly cupped and striking the fleshiest part of Jennifer's ass, the slap was deceptively loud, echoing in the silent room like a whip crack. It probably didn't hurt at all, but a shudder rolled through Jennifer's body like it had. Mei paused, letting her process the sensation.

To Mei's surprise, Jennifer's head immediately lifted and turned. One eyebrow was arched, her lips curled upward.

"Seriously? That's it?"

The playfulness shattered any inclination Mei might've had to adopt the usual chilly, unmovable pro Domme persona. If Jennifer wanted playful, then Mei would provide it.

She laughed. "Oh I see. You're a *brat*."

With her left hand, Mei grabbed Jennifer's ponytail and tugged until her head was tipped back, the full pale column of her throat bared so that Mei could lay her other hand over it like a collar. As Jennifer grinned, biting her bottom lip coquettishly, Mei felt the urge, faint and brief like a muscle twinge, to kiss her forehead. She shook it away.

"You want to be treated like a brat?"

"I want to be spanked until I bruise. Do you think you can manage that?"

Oh, could Mei.

She let go, allowing Jennifer's head to fall back onto her arms, and then Mei took her position again. This time when she slapped Jennifer's upturned ass, she did it hard. Not as hard as she was capable of, but hard enough that Jennifer's body heaved forward with the force of it and she let out a startled, "Ah!"

"Better?" Mei asked, but didn't give her the chance to answer before she was hitting her again just as hard. It pulled another cry from Jennifer's mouth that was followed by a hiss when Mei rubbed at her asscheeks, digging slightly into the pinkening skin. "How about that?"

Jennifer only had time to suck in a breath before Mei spanked her again, then again, until the pink had deepened to red. Mei's palm began to sting; sweat beaded on the back of her neck.

She paused, reveling for a moment in Jennifer's harsh gulping inhales, her shoulders heaving while she waited for the next blow. Mei shrugged off her suit jacket and tossed it aside, unbuttoned the cuffs of her shirt and rolled up the sleeves to her elbows. Jennifer turned her head to watch, sloe-eyed and flushed. Her bottom lip was swollen from being bitten.

And that hadn't even been the best, or worst, that Mei could do. She smirked, flexing her fingers and chasing away the lingering sting in her hand.

"Anything to say?" she asked.

Jennifer swiped her tongue across her swollen lip, making it shine prettily. When she answered, it was in a whisper. "Green."

*Good answer*, Mei thought.

She grabbed Jennifer's ponytail and looped it around her knuckles, drawing Jennifer's head back and making her back bow until she couldn't bend any farther; she was surely feeling pinpricks of pain in her scalp. "Let's see if you can take a little more this time, then."

Mei lifted her other arm and swung it down, just shy of as hard as she ever dared during a session. Jennifer jerked forward, although she couldn't go far with Mei holding her in place by the hair. Her cry was sharp but cut abruptly off when Mei struck her again, giving her no time to recover from the pain before piling more on. In minutes, her body was limp, kept upright only by Mei's unyielding grip, and her short cries had weakened into deep sobbing breaths. Her reddened ass had darkened even further, forming blotchy purplish bruises.

Finally, when Jennifer was shaking and her eyes squeezed so tightly shut that sweat was gathering in the little crinkles at the corners, Mei stopped. They remained there, both gasping like they'd just finished a long, rough fuck.

Mei's throat was dry, her arm aching. She couldn't feel her palm any longer, so flooded was she with adrenaline and endorphins. She uncurled her fingers, now as stiff and brittle as twigs, from Jennifer's hair.

"Green," Jennifer said, panting, before Mei even had to ask. "Green."

Delight, and maybe a hint of pride, bloomed in Mei's chest. She chuckled, still breathing heavily from the exertion. "Okay. The crop's just right here, leaning against the back of the chaise. I'm going to grab it."

She kept a hand on Jennifer's head while she did, grounding her, and Jennifer indicated her approval with a low, grateful groan.

The riding crop was Mei's most basic one: plain black in color, no cutesy shapes or decorations. The tip was small, leather and thick, which made it brutal if Mei put the right amount of force behind it. She liked the welts it left, especially on skin that already had a good dusting of color.

"I think you'll like this one," she told Jennifer. "The initial pain is sharp, targeted, but then it radiates. It'll throb for hours afterward. A bit knifelike, actually."

Jennifer moaned, high and reedy, and shuffled her knees wider, angling her ass up even more. Mei admired the sight: the blend of reds and blues and purples, as breathtaking as a sunset.

"Well," Jennifer mumbled eventually, "get on with it."

*Brat*, Mei thought, snorting. She stroked the hair at Jennifer's nape before she stood back, giving herself enough room to swing the crop. It sang as it descended, the thin plastic shaft slicing through the air, and the *slap* when it struck Jennifer's right asscheek was wickedly sharp. The flesh dinted and quivered. Jennifer's cry was as loud and beautiful as the sound of the crop. Mei waited, giving her the opportunity to experience the full spectrum of sensation.

"Oh god." Jennifer's voice was hoarse. She rocked backward, chasing the sting. "Oh my god."

"I'm going to do four more," Mei told her. She could have been persuaded to do more, if Jennifer wanted to push her tolerance that much, but Jennifer only nodded, her eyes closed, and murmured another, "Oh god," as she poised herself for another.

Mei took her time with the last four. Minutes passed between each stroke as she listened to Jennifer's ragged breaths and pained cries and even caressed the welts with the thumb of her free hand, feeling the heat and the swell and smiling to herself when Jennifer always moaned softly and pressed back into her touch.

After the final blow, the slap of the crop hadn't even finished ringing out before Jennifer's limbs gave. She collapsed with a violent full-body shudder and a low, throaty, "Unhh." Mei reacted instinctively, dropping the crop and climbing onto the chaise. She wound herself around Jennifer's slumped body and made hushed shushing sounds into her hair.

"Good girl," she said. As Jennifer squirmed and whimpered, Mei stroked her sides soothingly. "All done now. You took that so well."

With their bodies so close, the scent of sweat, cocoa butter lotion, and hair product was thick and cloying. There too, although much fainter, was the smell of arousal. Mei thought at first that it was in her head, just some sort of mental association being tapped into, but then it grew stronger as Jennifer wriggled and whimpered again.

And then Mei realized that Jennifer's hands were between her thighs, that she was touching herself. In the same moment, the narrow tunnel of Mei's attention, which had been focused solely on Jennifer and her reactions, widened, and she felt the heaviness between her own legs, along with the throb of her pulse and the dampness in her panties.

"Oh fuck." Jennifer's voice was weak and trembling; there was a note of awe, even rapture, in it. She moved her hips in little hitching thrusts, grinding herself against her hands. "Oh fuck."

Mei didn't think about it: she just cradled Jennifer even closer and rubbed her cheek against Jennifer's sweat-wet shoulder. The position crushed her groin to Jennifer's ass and dug her hip bones into the fresh bruises and welts. "That's it." Arousal was thick in her voice. "Go on. Make yourself come."

"Oh god," Jennifer groaned, and oh Mei could hear it now— the slick wet sounds of her cunt, a soft squelch with each pump of her hips. Jennifer let out a cry that rose sharply and then crested as her legs began to quiver.

Mei imagined what she would feel like inside, how warm and slick she would be, and in her mind saw herself reaching around Jennifer's waist and hooking a finger in her cunt, feeling the muscles flutter and tighten as she came. It took every bit of her self-control not to rub herself off right then against Jennifer's ass. She was crossing enough boundaries already just by holding her, by encouraging her.

Mei was a professional; she would remain professional.

After her orgasm, Jennifer seemed to drift, doing nothing but panting harshly and lying limp and dazed. Mei used the time to ensure that none of the wounds were too serious, to slather soothing cream on them and then to simply sit beside her on the chaise, stroking her hair while she came out of whatever head-space the pain had put her in.

Finally, Jennifer stirred, walking her knees closer to her chest and propping herself up on one elbow. Her once-neat ponytail was now a nest of bumps and flyaways.

"This, erm. This might have to be our last session," she said. Although Mei had intended to say the same to her, it took great effort to prevent her shoulders from sinking in dismay. "I...well, I thought going to a professional would keep me from getting attached, but...I might've been mistaken."

Mei breathed, staring down at her own creased and sweat-stained suit pants, debating. It took seconds for her to come to a decision.

"It wouldn't have to be a session. It could be a date, if you wanted. If you wouldn't mind dating a pro Domme, that is."

Jennifer sat up fully, her head cocked.

"Huh," she said. "Maybe." Her lips curved into a smirk, and her eyes gleamed with the same sort of amusement Mei remembered from their meeting at the coffeehouse. "So, for a *date...* what are your thoughts on knives?"

# EASY

Anna Watson

That night, Mister Benson chose me. He came down into the crowd, took my hand and led me away from the press of sweaty bodies. The members of Chicken à la King Drag Troupe encouraged audience participation, and I'd seen other folks get caressed and treated to lap dances by Fats Dominant, Sonny Boner, Captain Candy and Power Strip. This was my fourth time seeing the Kings, and this time, lucky girl, it was my turn.

It was hot up on stage, and I couldn't see the audience very well because of the bright lights. I could hear my friends screaming my name, though, and I was so nervous I almost jumped back down to join them, but Mister Benson had hold of my hand in a commanding grip. Tall and slender, he was wearing a Daddy cap, a leather vest over his white T-shirt, jeans and chaps, and some shit-kicking boots. He led me over to sit on a single bed, all frilly and pink, that had been wheeled onstage. Beside the bed was a nightstand with a phone, a deck of cards and a vase holding a single red rose on it. Grooving to the beat of the loud funk coming over the sound system, the rest of the

Kings presented themselves to me. Sonny Boner, his impressive package looking good in his bicycle shorts, gave me a friendly pat on the shoulder. Power Strip kissed my hand, so dapper in his striped zoot suit. Captain Candy brushed back his long hair so I could see the gold rings in his ears, and blew me a sexy kiss. Fats Dominant came to attention and gave me a snappy salute, handsome as hell in his sergeant's dress uniform. Mister Benson just looked haughtily into my eyes and then away, never letting go of my hand. I was so flattered by the silent, exaggerated way they were welcoming me, playing to the crowd like the yummiest treat had just been dropped in their midst. And the male, pussy-driven energy they were giving off was really sending me.

"We'll be back," Mister Benson whispered, his lips brushing my ear. "Don't go anywhere."

The Kings grooved off the stage and the lights went down, leaving just a spot on me. The music stopped and the crowd held its breath. This was the last number of the night.

I sat there feeling silly, but feeling turned on. This would be something I could tell the grandkids about: the time I'd been in a number with the handsomest, sexiest, most popular drag kings this side of the Mississippi. My friends passed me up a beer, which I chugged, then passed back. I took a deep cleansing breath. I was in for the duration. I wanted to be. But truthfully, along with the turn-on and the fun of it all, I was struggling with just the teensiest worry.

See, I have this problem. Or you could call it a talent. A gift. The thing is, I'm a seriously sensual girl. I swear that every-thing—smells, tastes, sounds, the way things look and feel—goes straight to the pleasure center in my brain. And from there, on down. See, I'm easy, is what it is. To put it bluntly, I'm the kind of girl who can come at the drop of a hat. You don't even have to be touching me. Once, I came in the movie theater watching Vasquez in *Aliens*. I came, clutching my fag friend's arm so hard he squealed, when we went to hear Leslie Feinberg read from

*Stone Butch Blues*. I've come listening to k.d. lang's alto croon, and from a lover feeding me just-picked raspberries, warm from the sun. Being pressed up against a butch in a crowded bar, the feel of her suit on my bare arm, the smell of her cologne? Oh, baby! I've come watching a super-in-love couple dirty dancing, and you better believe I came when Lynnee Breedlove ripped off her shirt at a Tribe 8 concert and I caught it full in the face. I still have that shirt, and if I lick it, I can taste her sweat. Makes me come.

Usually when I come like that out in public, no one notices. I mean, it's not like I start panting or screaming and thrashing around. It's kind of decorous and private, really: this utterly delicious, ladylike wave of sweetness, starting in my pussy and traveling all through my body. If you were watching, you might see me shiver a little, and my face turn red, like I'm blushing. No big deal. Usually. The thing is, I can't control when it will happen, and I definitely can't stop it once it starts. Up here onstage, on a bed with the Kings? With a spotlight trained on me? Oh, geez.

When the music started up, at first I didn't recognize the song. It seemed too slow for the Kings, who usually perform to fast, racy tunes. The telephone on my nightstand rang. It was Mister Benson, asking me if I was okay, and telling me to just relax and let the Kings guide me. He told me to stay on the phone, that he would be seeing me soon. At that moment, the vocals started. I sat there getting goose bumps as the Kings came out, one by one, moving slow and sultry, as Janis Ian began to pour her heart out in that quintessential teenage girl angst song, "At Seventeen."

I pressed the phone to my ear as my invented lovers approached me. The Kings weren't lip-synching; instead they moved sensually to the music, sexual fantasies called up from the depths of every lonely baby femme's girlhood. They preened and showed off, displaying their individual personas, inviting me to look, to take. Each man opened his heart and pulled out a piece of his soul to offer me in tribute.

Captain Candy knelt beside me and began running his hands up and down my legs, leaning down to kiss and fondle my high heels. I relaxed into the heat of his palms. Sonny Boner and Power Strip embraced and began to pull off each other's clothes, looking right at me and giving the awkward, small-town girl the thrill of her life when they ended up in just long white dress shirts with their strap-ons peeking out. Fats Dominant lowered himself to the bed, leaned against the headboard, and gently pulled me between his legs, my back to his big belly. Mr. Benson appeared and took the phone from my slack hand, hanging it up. He joined Fats Dominant on the bed and began trailing a little leather whip lightly over my body. The other three gathered around, touching my head and shoulders, my legs and feet, transforming me from ugly duckling to femme goddess.

The melancholy, haunting song went on and on, and the audience roared and whistled and hollered the names of their favorite Kings. I was sweating, my pussy swollen and moist and practically on view in the short skirt I was wearing. My breathing quickened and Mister Benson shot me a look. I shifted my bottom, pressing back into Fats Dominant and getting a good feel of his hardpack. The room started to spin. It was going to happen; there was no way of stopping it. I looked desperately around for something to help me, something to calm me down, but just ended up locking eyes with Mister Benson, who had the smallest of smirks on his handsome, cruel face. He cracked the whip, making me gasp. Then, very slowly, he brought out the tip of his tongue and touched it to his moustache. The red, glistening tip of his tongue flickered out once, then again. He lifted a finger to his mouth and sucked it, briefly, before drawing it lovingly down his body. His eyes never left mine for a moment. The boys surrounding me, sensing a change, began touching me more intimately as they swayed to the music, lingering on my calves, my ankles, my neck, my belly. I could smell their sweat, their cologne, the musk from between their legs. And I came.

It started with a quivering, deep-down flutter in my pussy, and I couldn't help it, I lifted my ass off the bed. The Kings had my hands and feet and I pushed up, up, my skirt lifting to show my wet panties as I writhed and moaned—this one was hardly decorous. I could feel my nipples straining deliciously against the material of my blouse, and I knew my whole body was flushing red with pleasure. I couldn't help it. I shouted. I came shouting Mister Benson's name, and just as things were getting really out of hand, the song ended and the curtain came down to thunderous applause.

The talk later was that it had all been planned. Most of the Kings didn't believe I'd really come—they thought I was a big exhibitionist who had concocted the whole thing to show off. Not that they were complaining, since it had been their most popular number ever. Before I left the stage that night, though, Mister Benson gave me a full-body hug, pressing his dick right between my legs and causing major aftershock. He handed me the rose from the nightstand along with his card, cell phone number scrawled on the back. Because Mister Benson? He knows an easy girl when he sees one, and that, apparently, is what Mister Benson thinks is just a little bit of all right.

# GRINDHOUSE

Valerie Alexander

The marquees of Times Square scream with light and color as I walk down 42nd Street. *Hellcat in High Heels* and *Space Invasion 56*, shrill the grindhouse theaters, advertising double, triple and all-night bills. Under the brilliant displays, the usual denizens of Times Square mill around the sidewalks: drag queens, hustlers, drug dealers, tourists, cops. One of the friendlier hustlers interrupts his transaction to holler "Cynthia!" my way. Most of the regulars know me by now, the dancer from the burlesque theater up the street who comes down here once a week or so.

It's a raw wet March night. The rain has just stopped and the wind feels good on my face after being in an overheated dressing room. My long brown hair is tucked under a cap, just in case any customers recognize me as a girl they've seen dancing in pasties, sequins and feathers. Burlesque might be a dying art form today in 1955 when anyone can buy girlie magazines or even see nudist colony films right here on the Deuce, as we call it, but plenty of Times Square trade have a foot in both worlds.

The 42nd Street subway entrance awaits down the block, beckoning me to my neighbor's party with his phony Beat friends. Or I could go to my favorite Village bar, where the possibility of a raid isn't as terrifying as the possibility of seeing my ex, Dee, slow-dancing another femme to heaven in her arms. But my mission tonight is more private. More exciting. Something no one knows about but me.

I head inside the Smokes & Curiosities Shop. Ignoring the furtive men flipping through magazines, I pick up the newest copies of *Frolic* and *Titter* and go to the counter with a pounding heart. The proprietor doesn't disappoint; he pulls out a newspaper from under the counter and opens it to show me a new issue of *Strange Ways*.

"Something special, if you're interested," he says. That's what he always calls it: something special. *Strange Ways* is so taboo it can't sit on the shelf with the other cheesecake magazines.

"Thank you," I say primly and pay for the magazines as if I'm not already squirming inside.

These pages aren't going to show me the cutie next door with her top off. They'll show the vamp, the bad girl, the cruel mistress and her trembling princess. Every issue is a black-and-white dream world of girls in corsets and stilettos, girls shackled in dungeons and menaced by strong women.

"Yep." Then he adds casually, as he gives me my change, "You know, this photographer Red Bosworth is doing movies too. There's one right next door at the Elysium Theatre."

It seems too incredible, the idea of my bondage girls coming to life. "Thank you."

Back on the street, the Elysium Theater entrance waits like an open, grinning mouth. *Cat Fight Confidential!* the marquee promises. *Pyromania!* The Elysium is one of the sleaziest theaters on the Deuce, crawling with hustlers and their scores in the balcony and plainclothes vice prowling the rows of seats. Supposedly a man got mugged in the restroom last week. But that doesn't stop me from handing my money to the girl behind the ticket-booth glass.

I settle in near the back. A black-and-white film set on a beach is playing, what they call a low-budget roughie. But just a few minutes later, a new film starts—these seem to be mostly brief film clips—and a flickering, black-and-white screen spells out *Cat Fight Confidential*.

This film has no dialogue, just a merry instrumental tune. A blonde society girl is brushing her hair at the mirror. A maid sweeps in and they argue. The hairbrush is snatched back and forth a few times, and then the girls are pushing each other and wrestling all over the floor.

I lean forward in my seat, scarcely able to breathe. The girls tumble energetically around the room until the maid gets fed up and pins the society girl on the bed, pulling off her dress while the society girls kicks and screams. I wait for them to grind against each other, for the maid to strip her naked. But she only brings the blonde down to the floor and pulls off her slip. The society girl twists and pouts in her bra and panties.

The door flies open and a tall black-haired woman strolls into the scene. She moves with a swagger, a jungle cat with a menacing smile. She scolds them both with much finger wagging, then holds up a length of clothesline. I cross my legs, flushed and excited. She's going to strip them naked and tie them up. All my life I've burned with dreams like this, secret shameful fever dreams of naked girls in bondage, and women who knew how to take charge.

But the tall black-haired actress doesn't pull off their clothes. Instead she swiftly bends the maid over the table—still in her uniform—and ties her hands to its legs, so the maid is stuck with her bottom sticking out. She ties the society girl to the other end of the table in the same position, then takes the hairbrush and begins spanking both of them with a smirk.

A shivery thrill snakes down my spine. She's so dominant.

So authoritative. My cunt feels hot and wet and swollen under my skirt.

The film cuts off and switches to a cowboy movie.

I can't get home fast enough. And my new issue of *Strange Ways* doesn't disappoint; there's a curvaceous blonde facedown in a leather swing, her hands roped behind her. On the opposite page, a black-haired girl is painting her toenails on the back of a bound and gagged woman. She appears two pages later in stiletto heels with a whip in her hand.

But the film. I can't stop thinking about it. About a different film clip, maybe, a girl in chains wiggling underneath me. Actually wearing those stiletto heels myself while that tall black-haired woman swaggers in and overpowers me, like a masterful owner who's going to fuck me good and hard no matter how much I pretend to struggle.

In the back of *Strange Ways* is the studio address.

"Welcome to the snake pit, Cynthia," says Red Bosworth the next week when I appear for my first scheduled shoot. Red, the photographer and filmmaker, is a woman, my first surprise. She's all business as she explains the rules of what she calls "fighting girl films," as if she films office supplies instead of partially undressed women getting paddled.

The movies are silent 8mm and 16mm black-and-white loops. Red runs me through the basics, which I've already gleaned: women in lingerie, latex and high heels performing in a variety of scenarios. The actresses dance, train slaves, lace each other into corsets and chain each other into bondage contraptions. No nudity; that's the rule. No sex acts either. Two pairs of panties must be worn, to block all pubic hair.

I don't understand why burlesque queens can bare their nipples onstage and cheesecake magazines can show topless girls, but filming two girls wrestling in their underwear is risqué.

"I mostly do a mail-order business, which means I send these

GRINDHOUSE

materials across state lines," Red says. "If this fits the definition of pornography, I could get brought up on obscenity charges. We have to be careful. Oh, here's Kathy."

The other actress is a little younger than me, maybe nineteen to my twenty-four—that's by design. She's the ingenue I'm here to tame in the film. With big dark eyes and dark bobbed hair, she could be Natalie Wood's naughty little sister. We run through the scene. She's making something in the kitchen and spills it. I come out, hands on hips, and express dismay. Her hands fly to her cheeks—*Don't punish me, no, not that!* —and then I have her over the kitchen table, ruffly checked skirt up to show her panties, and she kicks and squirms while I dole out twenty pretend whacks on her upturned ass.

She bends over the table so agilely. Her breasts are spilling out of her low-cut dress and her thighs under her skirt are soft, firm, flawless. I keep her pressed down with one hand on the small of her back. This is the first time I've touched a woman in months. I try to look unrattled, calm, as Red instructs us.

"Let's get started."

Once the cameras are rolling, my lust evaporates. The film lights are hot, hotter than stage lights. I'm nervous as I focus on making the right expressions and spanking Kathy without hurting her. But as she fake-struggles beneath me, as if I'm really restraining her instead of just lightly resting my hand on her, my blood comes alive. All I can think of is a naked girl writhing underneath me in real life.

"Cynthia, you're a burlesque girl, right?" Red asks when we finish the scene. "How about some dancing?"

I strip down to the bare minimum allowed on camera and then slowly get dressed. Sitting on an elegant dining chair, I ease black nylons up my legs, caressing my calves and thighs. Next comes the garter belt, the spike heels, the gloves.

"Keep stroking yourself," Red directs. "They like to see that. Just keep it clean." Finally, after I've smoothed and admired myself everywhere, Kathy puts on a McGuire Sisters record and I stand up and begin to dance.

"Good job," Red says as she pays me in cash. "You've got good stagecraft. Just make sure you keep your expressions exaggerated. Lots of visual communication."

Walking home under the streetlights, I think of my ex, Dee, seeing one of these films. I want her to see them; want her to watch the black-and-white ghost of me and realize the real me will never be hers again.

Over the spring, I work in Red's studio quite often. Sometimes I do films and sometimes pictorials for *Strange Ways*. Hogtied in a bikini, looking pleadingly over my shoulder; tied to a dancer's barre, helpless as a head ballerina looms over me. In one film I'm tied to a bondage table and hit with soft switches. It's ticklish but I toss my head back and forth and grimace as if fighting great pain.

One night in June, I arrive at a quiet studio. Red is in the back, reviewing a *Strange Ways* layout. I'm putting on the extra-scarlet lipstick required to show up on film when a confident Amazon strides in.

Her black hair is piled up high and matches her black cigarette pants and tight shirt. Heavy eye makeup gives her an imposing look. My stomach clenches as I realize she's the woman from the *Cat Fight Confidential* film I saw at the Elysium Theatre.

She smiles a cool smile. "I'm Anita but you can call me A.J."

"I'm Cynthia." My voice sounds nervous.

Her eyes rake me. "You're new to this, Red said. I hope you know how to put on a show, kid."

"She knows what to do, A.J.," Red says, emerging from the back. "Cynthia is a burlesque dancer. She's been a real quick learner."

We run through the paces. "Okay, A.J., you'll be tying up Cynthia with this rope. Hands behind her back, then she's across your lap. Cynthia, you're kicking and yelling. A.J. spanks you—"

"Through my underwear?"

A.J. smirks.

"Of course," Red says, shocked. "She can't do it bare—what else is there?"

I change into a leopard-print bra and panties, covered by a navy dress that looks normal but is fastened in the back in a way that's easy to tear off. Walking out of the changing room, I feel unusually vulnerable.

A.J. stops me. "Stockings too," she says. "I'm going to rip them off you and gag you with them."

Her green eyes hold mine mercilessly. But Red looks pleased so I go back and put the stockings and garter belts on.

I walk out and the cameras are rolling. A.J. looms up with that menacing smile and I instinctively step back. She grabs my wrist and pulls me forward, her smile deepening, and then I'm on the couch, fighting her as she rips the dress off, pretending to struggle more with it than she really does.

But it feels real. The weight of her, this strong woman pinning me against the cushions and pulling at my clothes. I'm already flushed under the lights. The dress comes off and I feel utterly naked, as if the leopard print underwear will dissolve at any moment.

A.J. undoes my stockings next. I try to cling to them out of instinct but she prevails and then she yanks me to my feet, winding one sheer black stocking around my wrists and stuffing another in my mouth, until I'm gagged and bound and at her mercy.

A.J. drops onto the couch and pulls me over her lap. *Wham,* goes her hand on my bottom. It doesn't hurt, exactly, but it feels undignified. This doesn't feel like acting, it feels like a real usurpation of power. She tugs my thighs open and leaves one hand between my legs as she spanks me, her fingertips lightly—accidentally—brushing the crotch of my panties.

I struggle. I rock my hips back and forth, as much to urge her on as to fight her. I'm writhing, physically begging her to touch me. Then, holding me by the neck, she moves me onto the sofa on my knees. We didn't rehearse this. But Red keeps filming as A.J. pushes my face into the cushions, hands still tied behind my back, and my ass in the air. Both pairs of my underwear have ridden up my crack but A.J. keeps spanking me. The hand holding my thigh keeps brushing my clit as I struggle, driving me closer and closer to orgasm.

"Wrap it up," Red says. A.J. finishes the spanking with a flourish, ending with one stiletto heel on my back to indicate her complete dominion.

"That looked good," Red says, shutting down the lights. "You two work well together. Next time we'll use the pulleys."

I'm so wet that my underwear is soaked. I feel almost stupified with longing as Red leaves us to change and lock up. Between the humid June night and the earlier lights, the studio is sweltering but I can't get off the couch.

The silence settling over us is profoundly loud. After untying my wrists and yanking out the gag, A.J. goes to the refrigerator in the tiny kitchenette and takes out two cold bottles of beer. "Your burlesque background is obvious," she says and hands me a bottle.

I stiffen. "What's wrong with that?"

She shrugs. "You play it safe. There's no heat. No risk."

That's a ridiculous thing to say after the scene we just filmed. "It's a movie about a woman getting a spanking."

Her eyes hold mine. "It's a movie intended to give someone a perverted, throbbing orgasm."

I lose the stare-off.

"You're going to need training if we put you in the pulleys," she says. "There's a difference between how something feels and how it looks. You have to express your pleasure to the viewer." She puts down her beer. "Come on. Let's rehearse."

I've avoided the pulleys until now. They're a complicated-looking structure of support beams, suspension cables and chains used for suspending models. To me they represent the utter loss of control. Other than having my wrists and ankles tied, I've not been restrained in the films. The idea of surrendering that level of control on film—being hiked up spread-eagled and taunted and spanked—is too close to my more shameful fantasies. The protesting, struggling and fighting are an acting job, no different from my burlesque performances. But actually living out my dream of being bound and controlled by a commanding woman on camera makes me panic.

"Come on, kid," A.J. says impatiently. "You heard Red—this is what we're shooting next time."

I walk across the studio, every step rooting me to the floor. My underwear is clinging to my pussy. My hair is tousled out of its careful style. I feel as vulnerable as a small monkey going to a jungle predator.

"I don't know how to do this," I say.

"Just stand still."

She attaches black leather cuffs to my ankles. Their cool smoothness sliding around my skin feels sexier than the clothes-line we normally tie each other up with. Two chains rattle across the floor as she links one to each cuff. I feel like her captive.

"Arms up."

My wrists are locked into similar black cuffs and chains. A.J. disappears behind me and then the rattle of the chains begins, the slack disappearing. Then it's happening, I'm being lifted off the ground. Suspended and spread, my ankles opening wider and wider.

A.J. stands before me and regards her handiwork. "You look stiff as a board. That's not what viewers want to see—they want to see you pout and look scared, but your body has to be fluid."

"How can I feel fluid when I'm stretched open and completely bound?" I can barely get the words out, I'm so nervous.

"I'll loosen you up."

She vanishes into the supply cabinet, and then emerges with an instrument I've never seen—strips of soft leather emerging from a firm handle.

She smiles when she sees my panic. "It's just a flogger. Don't worry, I'll play nice."

She trails the leather strips up and down my back. It feels sexy. Then there's a snap and a sting rockets through my skin.

The flogger goes down over my thighs. She flicks it so the leather strips dance over my skin, flailing it back and forth between my inner thighs until I shiver, tickling me until I'm biting my lip. The second snap of the flogger catches me off guard. But now the sting is almost pleasurable, like the bite of a dangerous woman. The toy dances up and down my back, the leather strips brushing my skin. Then A.J. pulls my underwear down, both pairs, and the flogger catches my exposed cheeks.

I cry out. It's different on my ass, not painful exactly but more significant. A statement of control, of ownership. At least the spread of my thighs stops her from pulling my underwear all the way off, a guarantee of both protection and frustration.

Suddenly her mouth is near my ear as she says, "The reason you're resisting is because you're still dressed."

Resisting? My body feels like hot, melting taffy. But A.J. rips my underwear off like she's stripped a thousand women before.

Having my pussy on display is a first in the studio. A.J. eyes me with a cagey smile, then undoes my bra and pushes it up, exposing my tits.

"What a shame not to get these on film." She flicks the leather ever so lightly on my bare breasts until my nipples are so stiff they ache. My tits feel bigger, warmer, prickling with heat. If only she would suck my nipples into her mouth. Instead she abruptly gives my wet and throbbing cunt the same treatment with the flogger. The leather skims my clit.

She laughs. "You are so wet." She tosses it behind me.

Her fingers move over my clit. For as expertly and forcefully as she handled me earlier, she's taking her time now and it is taking all of my self-control not to beg her to fuck me.

"*So* wet," she murmurs, as if to herself, and slides two fingers inside me. I groan, I can't help it, but she only fucks me a little, my cunt clinging to her fingers, before withdrawing and rubbing my own wetness all over my pussy. She's using her knuckles, her palm, to rub me up and down. No woman has ever used her hands on me like this, turning my pussy into a molten, thrumming pool of bliss.

She lightly bites each breast, sending an electric jolt of sensation through me. But then she slides around behind me and I almost groan with disappointment.

The flogger presses up against my sopping wet cunt again. She's not whipping me with it, though, but rubbing it back and forth, parting my lips, pressing against my clit, the soft leather feeling like an extension of her own skin.

A.J. bites the back of my neck. "You're made for this life," she whispers. Then something solid is pushing inside my lips: the flogger handle. She works it inside me, the unfamiliar thrust filling my skin with electricity. Her other hand slides around and covers my clit, toying with me and fucking me relentlessly in conflicting sensations that push me up into a crescendo of fire—and then I'm coming, my pussy clenching hard around the handle as I surrender in wave after wave of intense joy.

"Oh god. Oh my god."

My face is streaked with tears. A.J. lowers, unchains and unlocks me. I hang on to the pulley poles, exhausted and shaking, while she disposes of my torn underwear and cleans the flogger. I feel utterly dismantled. But I get dressed and we go down the rickety four flights of stairs in silence, me feeling naked beneath my skirt.

Out on the street it's another New York summer night. A

diner glows across the street. I muster the courage to ask if she's hungry.

But A.J. smiles her crooked smile and says only, "Nice working with you, kid." She vanishes down the sidewalk, under the streetlights.

I never worked with her again. I made thirteen more films—pillow-fighting, wrestling, dancing in a black bikini, taking baths—before Red was charged with indecency that fall. Spooked, I quit the burlesque and Times Square forever. On New Year's Day, 1956, I headed to the Greyhound station on 34th Street and caught a bus west to California to start a new life.

But first, on a snowy December night, I returned to the Elsyium Theater to see an all-night Bad Girl grindhouse bill. After two short clips, a movie called *The Wicked & The Wild* came on the screen, flickering its black-and-white 16mm charms. A.J. loomed enormous on the screen, the power of what I knew to be her green eyes mesmerizing as she pinned me on the couch and stripped off my dress. My face didn't look frightened at all, but besotted, incredulous. I looked like a girl who was getting everything she dreamed of in the form of a dominant woman mastering her on camera. As my cinematic double squirmed on A.J.'s lap, I felt it all, the heat and muscle of her, the confidence of her fingers. Sitting in that theater seat, I knew I would never be mastered by a woman like that again. And in the years to come, years of discovery and surprises and trails blazed, I was proven wrong in some ways as I met other comrades, and right in others as I remained haunted by her, even as the decades continued to pass.

# GIVE AND TAKE

Annabeth Leong

The musicians who came through the venue no longer gave me any thrills. Whether their drum kits, amps and guitars were cherished and protected or banged up and tossed in splintering cases, I handled the stuff with equal care, but I no longer looked at the girls themselves.

The Tuesday of the Shrinking Violet show didn't start out any differently. As a perk of the job, I could have watched the acts and had a couple of free drinks, but I planned to hang out backstage, plug my ears anytime I could get away with it and try to study for an upcoming network certification exam.

Violet sought me out personally to talk to me about her guitar before relinquishing it to my supervision. I made notes about how she wanted it treated and didn't bother to get more than impressionistic glimpses of a shimmery minidress, ripped tights, and boots that were probably more expensive than their scuffs and stains suggested. She asked for my name, but I didn't let the show of courtesy trick me into any belief in intimacy or friend-ship. It didn't seem worthwhile to pay attention to her face.

I did my job, and I managed to get through a few of my note cards while the warm-up bands played. Maybe it should have bothered me that I'd lost interest so completely in the creative fire that used to fuel my life, but I was too busy dreaming of a future working in offices where I wouldn't have to worry about eventual hearing loss.

One of the other techs nudged me, too hard for the gesture to feel friendly. "What the hell, Nikki? You're not going to listen to her?" The audience seemed unusually passionate. It produced cheers that sounded more Thursday than Tuesday to me. The first chords of Violet's show bubbled up from beneath the screaming.

I'd written them.

Violet repeated the riff, building it slowly toward a glory I had once known. She was working the crowd to greater heights as she flirted with flinging her set wide open, her voice lifting above static and raucous shouts. I shoved the note cards messily into the space between a stray amp and the wall, ignoring the few that fluttered free.

I couldn't help humming the notes that came next as I burst out of the spot where I'd been holed up and into view of the stage. This time, I looked right at Violet. Standard rock-star uniform, a well-cared-for but unremarkable guitar, that sort of pretty that's easy to Photoshop into the appearance of flawlessness. All that was what I expected—they don't send girls on tour anymore unless they look like that. But this time I saw how she relaxed when our eyes met, as if she'd been waiting for me. I saw the flare of her wide nostrils, the unusually big hands that made it look easy to form tricky chords on the neck of her guitar and the way she'd already begun to sweat.

She looked so young, but I'd been even younger during the wild six months I traveled the country forming those very same chords, singing to crowds that screamed just like this one.

Violet signaled her band, and the song started in earnest while the crowd quieted. I was ready to cringe, to hear amateurish mistakes in the songwriting that I wouldn't have noticed when I used to play this, but now the song seemed beyond my abilities, as if I'd discovered a trunk full of journals I'd written in a language I no longer spoke.

She was a great performer. In her throat, my song became hers. The air between us thickened with strange chemistry. The shape of the notes was mine, but the tone of them hers. A song that had slept for a decade roared awake, stretched its jaws wide and tore the breath from my lungs.

Fuck, I'd been angry when I was young. And unafraid of being sexy. Or maybe that part was her.

With each beat of the song and my pulse, I warmed with life, until the whole venue's heat pounded in my temples.

I remembered what it felt like to stare up at a woman and see her as a goddess. Before I learned to play, I watched women onstage—handling their guitars with effortless strength, kissing their microphones as they snarled or purred their songs, kicking cables out of the way as they strutted back and forth—and dreamed of serving them any way I could, even for a few moments. Did they want me to scream their names? To bow? To fall to my knees and dip my head between their legs?

Funny that when I was the one onstage, I still never felt like I was taking. I only knew how to give. I brought lovely groupies into motel beds and smiled at their jaded, clever talk when what I needed was sincerity. And when I let them eat me, it didn't matter how they looked up wide-eyed from the curls of my pubic hair, longing for approval. Whether they pleased me or not, they consumed me.

All that had ended for me a decade ago.

Before Violet could finish performing my song, I shut her out with my earplugs. Backstage, one of my note cards was missing and another had been crushed by several shoes. My hands shook as I tried to smooth it out and put my deck in order.

* * *

"You didn't like the way I played it?"

Even if the voice hadn't sent shivers of recognition and desire up my spine, only one person could have asked that question. I didn't look up. "You made it sound better than it ever did."

"Well, that's not true."

I sighed. False modesty never looked good on anyone. If the song hadn't sounded good when I played it, I'd never have been almost famous. I coiled the cable in my hands more rapidly, twitching it with impatient jerks when it hung up on uneven spots on the stage. "Shouldn't you be at an after-party? Or, if you're the responsible type, resting up in your motel?"

"I was going to invite you onstage. See if you wanted to join me for the last chorus."

"Why would you do that?"

The stage creaked under her boots as she squatted. Now that she was eye-level with me, I had to drop my head to the point of neck strain to avoid her gaze. "You don't know anything about me, do you?"

I cleared my throat. "A lot of musicians come through, you know."

"Yeah, different band every night. I get it." She sounded brave and angry, but there was a wobble underneath that finally tricked me into lifting my eyes to hers. Violet looked impossibly young and impossibly old at the same time, and the stage seemed to shift beneath me. I didn't want to see her as a goddess, but she was making me feel outside of time and uncertain of everything.

I whispered a little bit of the truth. "I sort of lost interest a while ago."

"No." She shook her head and tumbled easily out of the squat and onto the bare stage, catching herself on her palms and crossing her legs mid-movement. My eyes dropped without my permission. She made no effort at modesty. Through one of the rips in her tights, I could see a patch of lacy purple underwear.

It was hard not to look, especially when I knew her face would affect me even more.

Seeking refuge, I crawled halfway behind an amp and started on another cable. "You're saying I didn't actually lose interest?"

"People who lose interest are indifferent. That's not you. You're scared."

It felt satisfying to rip a piece of black duct tape off the stage. She wasn't exactly telling me things I didn't know. But she was trying to make me talk about things I didn't like to talk about. For a second, I fantasized about my future job in IT so hard it just about brought tears to my eyes. No more late nights in this beer-sour building. No more unpredictable encounters and loud noises. No more bitterness, and no more constant reminders of why I was bitter. No more jealousy.

No more gorgeous twenty-two-year-old rock stars who had for some reason taken the time to learn to play a song that only barely remained within the grasp of my own muscle memory.

"Why did you learn it? When did you learn it? Hell, how did you even know it exists?"

She coughed, the sound strange coming from the throat of someone so perfect looking. "That's one of my things. When Shrinking Violet tours, I call ahead to every venue, ask if they have any musicians in the house. I pick stuff to learn as a tribute. You'd be surprised—well, maybe you wouldn't be... *I* was surprised how many former and current musicians are working as techs and ticket-takers and bartenders and whatever."

I wasn't sure if the explanation made me feel more or less special about her having chosen my song. "How big of you," I said. The sarcasm in my voice made me wince.

"I'm not trying to be high and mighty. I'm just...aware."

"That in ten years you could be in my position."

"I didn't mean that in an insulting way."

"No, I get it."

"I don't think you do," she said, rising and walking into my line of vision. I found myself staring at a patch of pale pink knee through another rip in her tights.

The idea of her walking away now made me feel cold, as if her presence had been warming me even while I resisted it. "Hang on," I said. "How do people react to this thing you do?"

"Some of them are really happy and excited. Flattered."

"But not everybody."

"Some people are embarrassed of their songs. They tell me later that they don't agree anymore with the lyrics they wrote."

"And are some people assholes about it?"

"Oh yeah. Some people criticize everything about my performance."

"I'm not criticizing you."

"I didn't call you an asshole."

"I'm something, though, aren't I?"

"I already told you. Scared."

I wanted to prove I was brave. I wanted to stand up, grab a guitar and show her. Or maybe just skip ahead and grab her by both upper arms and kiss her until she knew how fierce I could be.

I did something even braver. I apologized. "I should have listened to your whole cover. Your whole set. I'm sorry."

The coldness went away in a rush. Violet returned to me, closer this time, sitting beside me. I relinquished what had become a death grip on my latest cable. Her thigh brushed the side of my knee. She smelled of sweat, but it was just salty, not sour. "Do you still play?"

"No."

"Why?"

The thing I liked talking about least of all. "I had a contract for a second album. I tried to work on it while I was touring. That song—the one you played—it was all I could do."

"It's a good song. That's why I chose it."

"It was the end, though."

"What do you mean? The end?"

"I ran out after that. I didn't have anything left to say."

"I don't believe that's possible."

"I wish it hadn't been."

We were quiet a long time. Her hand crept to mine. My stomach wouldn't stop churning. I'd never been more uncomfortable in my life, and I couldn't imagine this moment felt any better from her perspective.

"I see why you're scared," she said.

I shook my head. "I don't think you do. Not unless you know what it's like to feel completely and totally emptied out."

"But you weren't. You couldn't have been."

She wasn't a goddess. She was a kid. She was giving me that same wide-eyed look—the one I'd seen on groupies, the one I hadn't been able to recognize at first when I slept with aging rock stars. I couldn't understand why the hell she'd want approval from me, but then I remembered. At a certain point, it didn't matter where that came from as long as it came from somewhere.

I never did know how to take.

I brushed a lock of hair out of her eyes. It was so heavily styled that hairspray crackled against my hand in resistance. She relaxed into the movement, resting the side of her head in my cupped palm. It was like I'd never even tried to be anyone else. I knew just what she needed from me and how to give it to her.

Her words had been so challenging, so confident, but Violet's body melted into mine when I pulled her close. I could feel her trembling. I stroked the sweaty back of her head and glanced around the venue. Most people had gone home already, but there was always the chance someone in her entourage might come looking for her. As a musician, she needed discretion, even if she hadn't learned that yet.

I let her go and told her where and when to meet me. She

slipped off to wherever she'd come from. My chest had tightened, making it hard to draw a full breath. I didn't know if I was excited or terrified, but I finished my work in record time.

She'd tried to make herself look ordinary before coming over to my apartment, but the effect was anything but. Fame and talent have an aura, and now that she was trying to conceal that, it poured out of her eyes and flowed from her hair. Her ragged T-shirt emphasized the unusual tone of her arms, and her big sunglasses drew attention to the expressive lips she used in her performances. Now I didn't know how I'd managed to see her as part of a faceless line of acts parading through the venue. She clutched a guitar case against her side, as if this was a first band practice and she was nervous about it.

I let her in. The guitar case banged against the wall, and I took it from her and set it gently on the floor. I watched her look around the apartment, her eyes widening as she took in my schoolbooks and the walls bare of posters. She'd said she didn't mean to insult me, but I knew she was thinking about how desperately she didn't want to end up like me. She wanted music to be a part of her life forever. She wasn't the type to understand how I could let it go.

As for me, seeing her in my living room—the glamour that clung to her made the place feel more alive than it had in years. I tried to think of hoarse throats and unwashed bodies, the creaky, sandy feeling of nights spent without enough sleep, but in truth I missed the colorful darkness of people like her. I hadn't wanted to care whether she'd show up, but I'd been pacing for hours, watching videos of her songs on an app on my phone. If she left because of what I'd become...

I couldn't bear it. I showed her what I still remembered.

The first time I kissed a rock star, I thought she would taste pampered and expensive. But musicians don't get lives of luxury. Violet's lips were rough. Her tongue carried hints of the flavors of roadside diners. Her muscles felt ropy when I gripped her upper arms.

She kissed me back with familiar desperation.

When I let up, Violet was looking at me like I had some kind of answer.

"Maybe you'll be sorry about this in the morning," I said.

"I won't be."

"How do you know?"

She bit her lip and didn't say anything.

"Different venue every night," I said. "I get it." It was so stupid that this stung.

"You…"

I kissed her again before she could fumble for a compliment she didn't quite mean. I carried Violet to my bed.

Our clothes came off so easily—so much easier than all the other means I used to hide my nakedness. She had no tan lines anywhere.

I reached into my nightstand for my lube and box of gloves. Violet blushed.

"You don't have to use that."

"I do. I learned some things when I was on the road."

I spent a few minutes exploring her. It had been so long since I'd fucked like it didn't matter that I couldn't help touching her like I loved her. As I ran my palm lightly over her side and hip, then over the curve of her breast, just barely brushing the nipple, I glanced up at her face and noticed her chin trembling.

"It's okay," I whispered, and then kissed a path from her mouth to the corner of her eye, where I tasted a tear. "Tell me what you need."

She shrugged against my pillow.

"I'll wait."

I teased her with a fingertip, traveling from her hip bone to the very beginning of her mons but going no lower. She had thick black pubic hair, which surprised me. I'd thought everybody shaved these days. Maybe fashion had moved on while I wasn't paying attention.

Her hips rocked toward me, but I didn't take the subtle hint. Finally, she gave a little groan. "You're not going to fuck me?"

"Is that what you need?"

She lifted her head, wild-eyed. "You think I know what I need?"

"Then tell me what you want."

She grabbed a glove out of the box and pressed it into my palm. "I want to feel good."

I smiled a little. "Don't we all."

She rolled her eyes, and my cockiness slipped. I snapped on the glove. "What do you like?"

"Touch me."

Her cunt was so pretty, the palest pink under those dark curls. I wanted to make her swell and blush with arousal. I stroked her hooded clit, just saying hello, and stretched out beside her so I could kiss her while I did.

In no time, her hips were rocking again. I could feel her trying to direct my fingers to particular spots, but I resisted every time. I worked my other hand between our bodies so I could play with her nipples.

The position hurt my upper arm, but the discomfort was worth it because soon Violet was whimpering and sobbing into my mouth.

I grinned into our kiss. "You need something specific after all?"

"I need you to fuck me," she whispered through clenched teeth.

I pulled back, feigning surprise. "Why didn't you say so?"

She shook her head and laughed. "Maybe I'll call you an asshole after all."

"Sorry."

"Just do it, please." Her grin softened the exchange.

GIVE AND TAKE

She'd gotten very wet. With that plus the lube, my first finger slid into her with no trouble at all. I added another almost immediately, and I had to close my eyes a moment to savor her sweet gasp. Settling my thumb on her clit, I began to fuck her, watching the way her eyelashes fluttered and her body rocked as I moved.

My third finger made her head tilt back until I couldn't see her face. Her neck, though, was so long and lovely that I pressed a kiss to the side of it, and then nibbled down to her shoulder. Above me, she gasped and cursed and begged and prayed. I rocked back onto my heels and witnessed it all. I wasn't sure if she was with me or if her mind had taken her somewhere else, but I was with her.

Her cunt squeezed my hand so hard it hurt, and her clit hardened under my thumb.

My arm began to ache from the effort, but the moment I slowed, her head snapped up. "For fuck's sake, don't stop!"

I smirked and put more muscle into it.

Violet's legs spread wider and wider. She gripped my pillow with both hands and grunted with the effort of working herself up to orgasm. I didn't like that she was fighting so hard for it. I pulled my hand out of her with one smooth motion.

She flinched as if I'd slapped her. "What the—?" Her eyes were unfocused, searching the room as if she'd lost me along with her orgasm.

I waited. She scrabbled up to her elbows. "What's the matter?" she asked.

"Nothing."

"Then why did you...? That was mean!"

Gently, I returned my hand to her pussy, petting it. She whimpered and started grinding against it.

"I'm not trying to be mean. I'm just letting you know you've got plenty of time. I'm here all night. You don't have to strain yourself."

146

"I need—"

"Shh. I know you need something. But lie still. I want to try to give it to you."

Her cunt sucked my first finger in. She quivered as I stretched her. And the moment I started fucking her again, she tensed up and started struggling again.

Violet moaned from deep in her chest when I removed my hand. "You asshole!"

"Relax," I reminded her.

She was starting to figure out the game. She clutched her upper thighs with both hands but didn't move her hips.

"There you go," I crooned. "That's what I want you to do."

Her thighs shook. I fucked her harder than I had yet. My knuckles banged her entrance with each stroke.

"Please… I want you to… I want to…"

"Patience."

Her toes pointed and her knees locked. Her back arched as if her breasts were being yanked toward the ceiling.

Violet tore her hands free of her legs, clutched at the air and then covered her face. The air between us had changed. She wasn't trying to orgasm anymore; orgasm was starting to happen to her.

"Almost there, pretty girl."

She sobbed and came with all her muscles. I bit my lip as my cunt squeezed in sympathy with hers. I curled my fingers to draw out her orgasm.

I got so caught up in watching her that it took me by surprise when she lunged at me, kissing clumsily, clawing my sides, grabbing for the box of gloves.

"You don't have to…"

"Shut up."

She'd obviously done this before, but she didn't have finesse. Once inside me, her fingers searched blindly. Part of me wanted to resist her, to prove I knew her body better than she knew mine.

She was so eager, though, that I just surrendered to her. Amid her mess of kisses, there were lucky strokes here and there. Her hip brushed my clit as she fumbled, and I was coming, hard and unexpectedly, both of us laughing with disbelief. I drew her down for a slower kiss and realized there were tears in my eyes, too.

I never learned to take, but sometimes I've been given moments of strange, accidental grace.

The morning after I was with Violet, I woke up alone except for the smell of her hairspray and her sweat. Stumbling into the kitchen, mumbling to myself about coffee, I stubbed my toe against the guitar case she'd brought over the night before. I hopped and cursed, but then I sat on the floor and opened it up.

It turns out I wasn't completely and totally emptied out, after all. My fingers followed trails left by her fingers.

I've written a handful of songs since the night Violet spent with me—though I also passed my network certification exam. I like to think it means I never actually lost the music, and that she won't either. I like to think she left the guitar with me on purpose, to make up for the bit of my heart she took with her.

# MIRROR, MIRROR

Frankie Grayson

"You want to go in?" a voice to my side asked, and my stomach bottomed out because it was Rae's.

Around us, the carnival buzzed and whirled. I realized she meant the fun house I'd stopped in front of to check a text just before she'd appeared, close enough to touch and raising her dagger-sharp eyebrows at me, *Well?*

Well.

I'd wanted her for three months, since she'd first arrived at the community women's center where I worked in development. She was an almost-counselor, checking off internship hours toward her license on a rotation with our health services department, and had instantly become my chief workplace distraction. I'd pegged her for queer in Week One from the way we smiled at each other—suggestive at the edges, holding eye contact a beat too long. I'd tried to uncover if there was someone waiting at home with dinner. There never seemed to be, but Rae was as elusive as she was teasing. Keeping it office appropriate, I'd guessed.

It was her last week at the center, and that Friday coincided with a work team-building night at a carnival. I was doing a shit job of building anything with my team; all evening, I'd been imagining getting Rae on her own since we suddenly, technically, no longer worked together.

I scanned the fun house. Standard county fair kitsch, one of those fold-up, clanging metal horrors painted on its front with a goofy theme. This one seemed to be generic fairy tale, with a knight sword-waving at a dragon and a wispy blonde princess fainting on the sidelines. But the doorways were dark, and it seemed almost creepily deserted, the crowds lured away by flashier attractions. We'd be alone.

I took a breath. "I'm game if you are." I paid for my entrance and hers, handing a pinch of tickets to the slouching kid manning the door and feeling a little thrill at how the gesture made things feel more date-like. At the way Rae smirked, pleased and knowing, when I did it.

Dim, colored bulbs lit the passages we crept down. Jets of air burst from unseen vents, or the floor gave way to rollers, leaving us laughing and grabbing hands for balance. Rae's laugh was like her voice: smoky, languid. Killer.

Then came the obligatory room of trick mirrors. In the first, we were all crazily stretched legs and even then, proportioned like a heron, Rae had my mouth watering. But I also noted what I had from the beginning, that she and I actually looked alike. Hair dark and jaw length, hers curly, mine straight. Similar lines to our faces, same build and height.

Initially, it had felt almost weird to be attracted to her— would she diagnose me as a narcissist, if I were her patient? But the boil in my blood told me this wasn't self-worship; I wanted to worship *her*, toes to tits to teeth. Rae was also prettier, no false modesty, and wore "our" features perfected. I was a jeans-and-T-shirt girl. I liked boots. I'd throw on some brown eyeliner when I had to meet with a donor but mostly didn't think about how I wanted to look. How I wanted to be.

Rae, on the other hand, was stunning, all business hard-ass with a very feminine edge. Silky camisoles peeking from chic blazers, dangerously sharp pencil skirts with the attitude to match. That night she wore a tight sweater and even tighter jeans. Black kohl on her eyes and lips painted red as a candy apple. Or a poisoned one.

In our reflection, Rae watched me watching us. "You like mirrors?" she asked. Instantly I thought of how we'd look in some glassy surface, tangled—my head between her curvy thighs, the fall of her breasts as she leaned over me—and swallowed hard.

"Depends on what I'm looking at," I said. We stepped to the next mirror to catch each other's gaze, finish the volley of flirtation, and busted up when our eyes blinked back big as dinner plates.

"Come on," she said, pulling me along by the hand. The walls of the next passage were all glass, and then we took a corner and were swallowed by mirrored angles. A maze.

We wove around turns and backed out of dead ends. Whichever way you looked, there you were, but different sides—in profile, the back of your own head. It was dizzying, seeing all of myself at once, and my heart beat faster. Or maybe that was just Rae, and the scent of her finally, finally right there.

We hit another end, and I turned to get out. But Rae just stopped, only inches between us, and then backed me up until my head softly tapped the glass. From every angle, I stared at myself over Rae's shoulder, twelve of me, twenty. An infinity. And an infinity of Rae, facing me. My pulse going wild.

Watching me intently, Rae tipped her head. Considering something. Then she said, "So when do you want to go out?"

"Um, Sunday?"

"Where's your phone?"

I pulled it from my pocket and handed it to her. She whisked her fingers over its lucky face and gave it back. "You have my number."

Then she leaned in. Her hair whispered over my cheek. Her lips pressed softly against the side of my neck, with that slight, maddening point of wet at the center that cooled instantly as she pulled away.

"So Sunday," she said, and turned. I followed her. She seemed so sure of where she was going.

And she was. She led us directly out of the maze, the end of the fun house, and turned to wink at me just before she disappeared into the jostling crowd. It wasn't until later, undressed, that I saw in my own bathroom mirror what my shirt collar had concealed: the perfect stain of her red lips on the side of my neck. Like I'd been marked.

When we texted over the next couple of days, it was to up the ante with hints of how we were going to basically wreck each other. So when I got one saying, *Can't wait to see you tonight. A request? Please dress femme for me. Your girliest, if you dare*, I was surprised—was that her thing?—but ready to bring it. I could dare if she could. Little black dress, glossy lips. I even busted out one of my two pairs of lace-waisted panties, which, because they were black, managed to match my only push-up bra, hallelujah. I sexy-messed my hair and, nerves prickling, waited like a good girl for her to arrive. She'd asked to pick me up—as if she hadn't been doing just that since we met.

A text buzzed in. *I'm out front.* I clipped down the stairs of my building, assuming she'd be waiting at the curb. She was, but the sight of her stopped me cold on the sidewalk.

Rae leaned against her car in the streetlamp light, smiling wickedly, in full drag.

So this was the game. I'd still play. I pulled it together and did my best saunter up to her, hyperaware of my clicking heels on the pavement. Ran my eyes up her tailored suit pants and a finger down the lapel of her charcoal jacket. The only makeup she wore was a touch of mascara on those long lashes. Her lips were as naked as I wanted the rest of her.

"Shall we?" she asked in that phone-sex voice of hers, opening the car door, and I let her hand me gallantly in, completely unsure of where we were going in every sense possible.

Our date was classic bordering on cliché. Candlelit restaurant, good bottle of wine (which she poured, like a gentleman). The verbal conversation was mere backdrop to the one our bodies had. She spent dinner running the toe of her wingtip up my calves, and when we pulled our chairs close to share a dessert, she snuck a hand under the tablecloth to skim her fingers along my bare thigh, to the edge of my skirt. Stopping.

I would have sworn I teased her back just to take the dare, to play into the competition that lent an edge to our courting, but acting the femme fatale started to feel surprisingly easy. Surprisingly good. I bit my lip when I laughed, like a reflex. I leaned to offer a view of my cleavage, breathing deep whenever her eyes caught on where I swelled out from my dress. When she picked up the check I felt with a dirty little thrill like she was buying me for the night, and more than ready to provide the services purchased.

In the car, Rae didn't ask whose place to go to. I silently let her make a couple of turns out of downtown and to wherever she wanted. I should have guessed I was in some kind of trouble by the way I had fallen pliant, supplicant—all those terrible descriptions of female abandon from shitty romance novels. But I could feel it: I would let her do anything to me for the night. She looked so damn good, hand capable on the steering wheel, jacket tailored to the nines. That pretty, pretty face in profile.

When she shut her front door behind us we fell against it together, no cues needed, to bite and lick the other's kiss, hands already everywhere. She worked so far under my dress to squeeze my ass, my skirt bunched around my hips. I pushed her jacket off and she ordered, "Bedroom."

The switch she flipped turned on only her bedside lamp, lighting everything in a soft peach glow. Her bedroom was just like her, unfussy yet ornamental, with exotic flourishes against competent practicalities. You could definitely tie someone to the bed's footboard, with its carved-wood slats.

But I wasn't there to admire her decorating. I undid her pants and she stepped out of them, leaving her in just her button-up with those miles of smooth leg beneath. She sat on the bed, pulling me to stand in front of her and sliding my dress from my shoulders, revealing my nonsensical bra. She cupped me, pressing the prickly-edged lace into my skin and running her thumbs over my silk-covered nipples before leaning in to nip them with her teeth. Wondering if she saw the goose bumps she conjured all over me, I slithered the rest of the dress down my hips, then shrugged my feet from my heels. I probably could have made a better show of taking them off, bending over to slowly unstrap them, but I was nearly shaking with hunger. I needed us both naked and grinding and coming. Now.

Then she dipped a foot under her bed and slid out a hatbox. More conjuring. Flicking the lid off with her toe, she leaned down and began to pull out its contents, and I laughed like some silly coquette when she produced a leather harness and then, a healthy-sized cock.

As she sat back up I slung a leg over her lap and lowered myself so our thighs slid and stuck. Toying with the shirt button at her throat, I all but purred. "So you want to fuck me, huh?"

She unhooked my bra and let it fall to my elbows, giving my neck a long lick, her tongue hot, soft. Said, "No, you're going to fuck me. You up for it, stud?"

For the second time that night, I froze.

It wasn't the request—it was the context. I'd strapped on, sure, but always with steady girlfriends, when we were both comfortable enough to drive each other like cars and, admittedly, needed some extra oomph in the bedroom. I didn't do it the first time I hooked up with a woman. And definitely not after I'd spent the evening tripping around town in my hottest come-fuck-*me* heels.

I suddenly had no idea what part I was playing in the night's bedtime story. Why had she dressed me up? Why hadn't she led some hard-muscled, well-hung butch back to her lair? I felt flustered, and knew that was the point from Rae's smile, which was all triumph topped with a femme's heavy-lidded bedroom eyes, the ones she'd been hiding for hours behind her suit and swagger.

From her box of tricks she'd also pulled out lube and a small bullet vibrator. She slid the toy into a pocket at the harness's front, asking, "Have you ever come inside a woman before?"

I shook my head *no*, mouth too dry to speak. But through my queasy nerves some other feeling was building—curiosity. Want.

Rae wrapped a hand around the back of my neck and nuzzled my face with hers. "Well, tonight you're going to. I want to watch you empty out into me." She matched her tongue on my earlobe to a dance of fingers over my clit, which was pressing against the lace of my lovely lady panties like the most aggressive hard-on. I meant to say, *Can we talk this over?* or even *Okay*, but instead made an animal noise and took her mouth in mine, shoving her back onto the bed.

She rolled my underwear off and the harness on in a few expert moves. My hands shook as I worked the buttons of her shirt, starting at the top. She began to unbutton at the bottom so we met in the middle and both undid the last one at her sternum, fingers tangling, and parted the fabric. Her bra was silky and red as that mark she'd left on my neck. I kissed her breasts, her belly, trailing down and lapping at the mound beneath her perfectly matched, ruby satin panties.

She gasped but gently pushed me from her. "Not here," she said, standing and shrugging her shirt off. My premonition about the footboard had been right in a sense. She led me to it and pressed her back against its rounded wooden edge to face me. "Here," she said, brushing my lips with hers.

I peeled down her underwear and we both gasped when my fingers hit the slick of her, hours-thick with desire. While I stroked her she retrieved the cock from the mattress and tugged the harness ring away from my body to slide it through, giving it a quick shot of lube as I tightened the straps.

She perched her ass on the edge of the footboard, just enough to anchor herself, and lifted one leg to spread herself open, placing her foot on my calf. "Are you ready?" she asked, and I didn't answer; there was no point. I was and I wasn't and she knew that. The fingers of one hand still behind the ring, she expertly flipped the vibrator on as she slid onto the cock.

The vibes crashed into my clit, perfectly timed with the feel of gliding along the tight, slick walls of her, a direct link between her body and mine, between my body and the cock. No, *my* cock. I choked out a cry and forgot to be careful, pushing all into her in one stroke. But she was just fine. Her head fell back with a pleased, throaty moan. I wanted to hear her repeat it. I drew out and pushed in again. And again. She grabbed my face and mashed her mouth into mine, muffling her yelp.

We fucked trading breath and sounds, me bending deeper in the knees until I was almost lifting her with each stroke. Rae kept one tiptoe anchored to the ground—I had grabbed her raised leg behind the knee and slung it high around my ass, where it scraped the harness strap into my hip bone as she ground onto me.

Then she stilled, and slid me out.

The wet of her glinted on my cock, and seeing it, I felt like a fish that had been tossed out of water. I'd die if I wasn't in her element. But she quickly turned, giving me her back, and bent forward to rest her elbows on the footboard so her cunt tipped up to me as an invitation, slippery, begging. I cupped her smooth ass with my palms and fitted myself into her again, and as I started thrusting, slid my hands into that great notch where a woman's thigh meets her belly. All the better to hold on to you by, my dear.

It was easier to fuck like that—or should have been. But soon, I couldn't catch my breath. The vibes I was packing were killing me. I rode torturous rises and plateaus, and through the delicious agony a worry pulsed in my head: that it was terrible for her, that I wasn't fucking her properly. I felt like I was spasming and then stopping still while every muscle in my pelvis tightened almost unbearably in response to the relentless titillation. I made noises I hadn't known my throat could produce.

On a cresting wave I gritted my teeth, and when it broke my fingers tightened around Rae's hips as I buckled and dragged her farther onto my length. And I heard her pant, "That's right, baby, yes. Like that."

I opened my eyes; I'd squeezed them shut. I saw Rae's head turned to the side, gaze locked feline-sure on something to our left. I looked.

We were framed like a painting in a full-length mirror hanging on the wall, showing feet to heads and every sweating, trembling, curving inch between. All of Rae's unbelievable inches, her belly swayed with the arch of her back, luscious tits still held up by her ruby bra. Center of the reflection, our hips met, my pelvis smacking into the swell of her ass and every moment captured in the glass and thrown back to us.

Like lock gears slipping into place, I suddenly understood what she had said earlier. *I want to watch you empty out into me.* She wanted to play her own voyeur. And consume me by sight.

So this was the game—I'd still play. Watching our private live movie, I ran my hand up her side just to see what it would look like. It looked damn good, her in my hands. Me fucking her with me.

That ripped me out of my head, and suddenly, the intensity on my clit was exactly what I needed. I pushed harder to feel more, thrusting steadily with one hand on Rae's hip, the other hooked over her shoulder, holding her tight in place against me. She moaned long and high while in the mirror, the muscles in my sides and ass clenched in bands, shuddering and tightening as I moved. My body looked powerful but vulnerable, controlled yet unhinged. I looked strong. I looked utterly helpless against what I was feeling, against what she made me feel. And I saw what she was so into, sketching and re-sketching my body and what I could be in it through her gaze.

Our eyes met in the reflection, and her creeping half smile told me she knew that I saw. She reached a hand back over her shoulder and, reading her mind, I took her fingers in and sucked, getting them good and wet. She plunged them between her thighs and I could see her take the rhythm she needed in the movement of her wrist at her belly. Her own mouth was fallen open, her brows knitted, but she kept her eyes on me in the mirror, drinking, roving. I gripped her breast, kneading as the pressure in me built again, Rae urgently whimpering *yes* on every stroke I pounded into her.

She rose onto her toes, knees straightening helplessly as her final build flexed through her thighs and ass, and then cried out, her cunt wringing my cock, tugging me deep into her against my stroke. That sent me over the edge. I curled over so my cheek pressed to her spine, and I rushed out, everything in me pouring into her. Never taking our eyes off us.

We breathed, Rae trembling beneath me. Shakily, I leaned up and pulled out the vibrator, switching it off and dropping it to the carpet at our feet. Rae rose, too, pressing back against me with her head on my shoulder, bathing my sweat-streaked face in her damp hair.

"Hey," I said, suddenly shy, feeling like someone new. Someone who needed introducing.

She gave my bottom lip a bite. "Hey yourself. How was that?"

I didn't know how to answer. It seemed like I'd been kissed awake after a long sleep. I dragged my hand up her thigh, mouthed her shoulder. I wanted more but didn't know, any longer, where that would take me. I studied our matched hips in the mirror, hers bare and soft, mine crossed with leather. The ways we were similar and how we were so different.

Rae watched me watching us. "What do you see?" she asked.

I shook my head—like *Nothing*, or *I don't know*—but said the truth. "Everything."

# THE ROAD TO HELL

Cheyenne Blue

Eve drives as if the devil is after her, chasing her along the interstate. Off to Colorado. The sun slants low, bruising the dry landscape with a golden glow. The color reminds her of Murphy, their Labrador, who no doubt is sprawled on the couch, his head in Teri's lap.

Eve's heart skitters like a rabbit, making her lightheaded. She sweats a film of nerves even though the air-conditioning is on high.

She's going to lose her virginity. That's what it feels like, even though she technically lost that nearly twenty years ago, the day Teri cornered her in the storeroom of the bakery where they both worked on Saturdays, kissing her sweetly and stickily, touching her in places that took you straight to hell. On that day, age seventeen, going to hell seemed a long way off.

Hell seems closer now. She's driving to Denver to commit adultery. She's going to kiss another woman, touch her, lie with her and find out how she tastes.

"I could come too, honey," Teri had said, as Eve flung jeans and shirts into a sports bag with pretend haphazardness—clothes she'd carefully picked out the week before.

Eve had given her a quick kiss and put as much sincerity as she could manage in her voice. "I wish you could. But it'll be dull. Talking food."

"Imagine if you get the contract!" Teri's enthusiasm was genuine, and Eve felt a stab of remorse. There is no contract. There is no company in Denver wanting to distribute her line of preserves. There's only a woman she met on the Internet and the allure of the forbidden sucking her in with silver tentacles.

Eve imagines she's dying, imagines she's facing her maker. It will be a dusty plain, where the land is as unforgiving as the god who made it. She imagines he can prize open the crannies of her mind so the cold plains wind blows her secrets out to paint the landscape. He'd say to her then, at the moment of her death, "Why did you not do it? Why did you not taste another woman? You wanted it so much."

Eve knows the god will shake his shaggy head, and pity her for her denial, even as he elevates her to heaven.

But after tomorrow, she'll go straight to hell.

She negotiates the Denver rush hour, weaving across the lanes of I-25 to take the downtown exit to find her hotel.

"They must think a lot of you," Teri had said, impressed, when Eve told her where she was staying.

"They probably put everyone up there." The lie rolled easily. It scared her a little, how good she is at the lies.

She wanders through her room examining the toiletries, the minibar, the wide-screen TV. *Teri would like this*, she thinks, but suppresses the thought. Teri is outside these two days of her life, which are moments out of time, an alternate reality. Afterward, she will return to Wyoming and live happily ever after with Teri.

They *are* happy, that's the thing Eve finds strangest in all of this. She doesn't want to change her life; she just wants a yardstick to measure it by.

She's too wound up to settle. She takes a swift shower and dresses in worn jeans and a white T-shirt. There's two hours before she's due to meet LeeAnn—time enough for a beer.

She finds a bar, sits by the window, and watches the people parade past: cowboy boots, bright shirts, and the smart black suits of office workers. Denver is an uneasy city, she thinks, not quite cow town, not quite metropolitan. She turns to share that observation with Teri, and she's three words into the sentence before she remembers Teri isn't there.

The dark woman who sits where Teri should be lifts an amused eyebrow when Eve apologizes. "Don't worry, honey, I do that all the time. Is your partner joining you shortly?"

There's a not-quite invitation in the gender-neutral words and Eve is surprised. She knows every lesbian by name in the small town where she and Teri live. All eight of them. She's forgotten it's different in cities.

"No," she says. "I'm here alone. On…business."

The woman smiles. "Welcome to Denver. May I buy you a drink?"

There's a subtle flirtation in the other woman's voice, in the closeness of her hand to Eve's on the counter. Laughter bubbles inside her. She's here to meet another woman, and in minutes a stranger is chatting her up. A very attractive stranger, she amends to herself. "What about your partner?" she asks.

The woman inclines her head. "I should have said I *used* to do that all the time. My partner died two years ago. But sometimes I still turn to where she'd be to share something with her."

"I'm sorry." The words are inadequate, but what else is she supposed to say? "I'd love a drink. Pale ale, please."

The woman signals the server, and then holds out her hand to Eve. "I'm Justine."

Eve introduces herself, and takes Justine's hand, holding it for three heartbeats too long. She's practicing flirtation, because it's been so long since she tried the moves—the tilt of the head, the slow smile. It's different on the Internet, where she has the veil of anonymity and can be someone she's not. Until later this evening when she is to meet LeeAnn, the not-quite-stranger. LeeAnn is blonde and statuesque, with a figure like a model in a men's magazine, and she wants to eat Eve's pussy, to munch it. She's typed the words in private chats, words that have Eve snaking her hand into her pants to bring herself off with short, quick rubs, fearful of Teri catching her.

Eve tries the head tilt and the smile on Justine to see if it works, and is rewarded with a flicker of Justine's eyes down to where her breasts barely swell the white T-shirt. The pale ale arrives and Justine's gaze breaks when the barman sets it down.

Justine smiles, slow and knowing. "Here's to new friends." She clinks her wineglass against Eve's beer and drinks as her gaze seeks out Eve again. "So tell me, Eve who is not from Denver, what is your business?"

For a second Eve thinks she's been caught, that Justine knows there is only dirty business. Her smile freezes as she realizes Justine's noticed the hesitation.

"You said you were here on business," Justine clarifies. "I'm asking what it is you do." Her direct stare seems to pick Eve's true intentions out of her brain. "Are you an accountant? Maybe a vacuum salesperson." Her smile makes it obvious she knows Eve is neither of those.

Eve hesitates. Hide the truth, she thinks, evade, tell lies if you have to. "I sell handicrafts," she says, in an approximation of the truth.

"That you make?" asks Justine. "You and your partner at home, maybe?"

"Something like that." Eve's short in her reply; the paranoia about what she is really doing in Denver puts rudeness in her voice.

"It's okay, honey," says Justine. "You can keep your little secrets." Her smile is feline, and she places a hand on Eve's

THE ROAD TO HELL

leg. "I don't know who you are, or what you're really doing in Denver, but I thought you might be open to some...company." Her fingernail drags small circles on Eve's thigh.

Eve sees knowing in Justine's dark eyes. As if Justine has been in Eve's position, sitting, jittery and on edge, about to do something that puts everything that is precious on the line. The urge to confess rises in her throat. Justine is not her god on a dusty plain, but Eve wants some sort of judgment. Maybe Justine is a smooth swinging city woman, who will laugh at the insignificance of what Eve plans. Maybe she and her partner had an open relationship, sucked and fucked with strangers. Or maybe she's a church lady, bound to her partner until death did them part, and she'll demand they drop to their knees to pray.

"Actually..." The neutral look on Justine's face encourages her. "Teri and I have been together all our lives. But I'm here to meet a woman I know from the Internet." She steals a glance at Justine. Her expression—open, encouraging—makes her forge on. "I've never slept with another woman in my life. Don't get me wrong, I love Teri, but I want to know what it's like with someone else."

"You could have gone to a sex worker."

"True, but that's not for me. I need a connection with someone. I met LeeAnn in a lesbian chat room. Physically, she's everything my partner is not. She's tall, blonde, immaculately presented. She knows it's just for one night, she's okay with that."

"And then you'll go home and carry on as normal?"

"Yeah. That will be the end of it."

"Will it? What if it's just the start?"

"No." There's conviction in Eve's voice. "I won't let it be. I love Teri. She's my soul mate. This is a one-time deal."

"What about guilt? Will you be able to look Teri in the eye?"

"I don't know," Eve admits, "but I still have to do this." She looks down at her hands, wound tightly together in her lap.

Justine's fingers still rest on her thigh. Eve could stretch her own fingers and brush them across Justine's, but she doesn't. Things are complicated enough. "LeeAnn wants to do things to me that Teri won't. She wants to use…toys. And she wants to munch my pussy. Teri loves going down on me, but that word, 'munch,' it conveys such enthusiasm."

Justine is silent for a moment, then she says, "When are you meeting LeeAnn?"

Eve checks the time. "In about twenty-five minutes. I should go. I have to get back to the hotel."

Justine stands. "I'm coming with you."

Startled, Eve stands as well. "There's no need for that."

Justine's dark eyes are inscrutable. "I think there is. You need someone at your back. Don't worry, I won't interfere, but not everyone is as they appear on the Internet. You meet LeeAnn in the bar. I'll be sitting across the room. If you like what you see, I'll leave after thirty minutes. If you don't, then you can make an excuse and come and join me."

Eve hesitates, but Justine's words make sense. But she's only known Justine for less than an hour—she's known LeeAnn for months. It will be okay. "Come on then."

They don't speak as they walk to her hotel. Eve gets a drink at the bar—red wine, not pale ale—she wants to look sophisticated, and besides, too much beer and she'll be peeing all night. She looks around. LeeAnn isn't here yet; there's a couple in one corner, two businessmen deep in conversation at the bar, and a man reading *The Denver Post* alone at a table. No LeeAnn. Eve settles into a chair where she has a clear view of anyone who enters the bar. Out of the corner of her eye, she sees Justine doing something on her phone at the bar.

The minutes tick on. The businessmen leave, the couple order food, Justine is watching the Rockies game on TV. The man is watching her over the top of his paper, she realizes. She looks away to discourage his gaze. Her glass is empty, and it's twenty minutes past the time when she was to meet LeeAnn. Eve orders another glass of wine. As the server sets it down, the man folds the paper and leaves it on his chair. He rises, and walks across to her, stopping in front of her chair, uncomfortably close.

Eve looks up, and lets her glance flick away dismissively.

"Eve?" the man says. "I'm LeeAnn."

She remembers little of the next few minutes. There was a blur of raised voices, of red wine roiling in her stomach, and anger lighting her blood. There was the slap, startling and sudden, his red cheek, her shaking legs. Then there was Justine, her hand underneath Eve's elbow, urging her to leave, asking for her room number.

When her mind clears, she's sitting on the edge of the big king bed for which she had such hopes. Justine emerges from the bathroom, presses a damp washcloth into her hands.

When Eve can speak without her voice shaking, she says, "I guess it serves me right." She looks at Justine. "Did you know? Or guess?"

"A bit of both. When you said 'munch' it sounded familiar. It's an unusual description. Then I remembered something online about a man who posed as a lesbian to pick up lesbians. He used that term."

"What's the point of that?"

Justine shrugs. "Power? The age-old idea that a lesbian is just a woman who hasn't met the right man?"

"I feel so fucking stupid." Eve's voice is small, weak. She can't think of the past weeks without shame—mainly that she was so stupid, falling for the oldest Internet trick in the world. The buzz of arousal that shaded her actions for the past weeks has withered and died.

Justine sits next to her and takes Eve's hands in both of hers. "Don't beat yourself up, honey. It happens. You're not the first, you won't be the last."

"Maybe, but it's the last for me. No more chat rooms, no

more cybersex…" She shudders, caught in the falseness of it all. "That man, getting off on… I'm going home tomorrow. I'm obviously not cut out for adultery." The god on the plain will send her to hell, for her intent was there, even if there was no action. And Teri…the guilt will come. She will go home and give Teri all the love in her heart, too wracked with the guilt of her betrayal to consider straying.

She just wishes she had experienced something to make that guilt worthwhile.

Justine shifts, and takes Eve's hands in her own, leans in and kisses her. Her lips rest on Eve's, a breath of hesitation. Eve feels the curve of Justine's lips as she smiles. Justine stays still, their mouths touching, their hands entwined. There's an offer in the kiss, an offer to salvage something of the evening. With a thrill, Eve realizes she's considering it—more than considering it. She wants it, wants Justine with an urgency. It's not just the situation, or the timing, or even the knowledge that it's now or never; Eve feels free again, and the thrill beats an urgent tattoo in her belly.

She deepens the kiss, parting lips, seeking with her tongue. This is the only woman she's kissed since Teri, only the second woman she's kissed in her life. There's heat and the taste of red wine, but it's how Justine kisses that sets her alight. She kisses deep, and the taste and feel of the body under her hands take her breath.

Justine breaks the kiss and arches an eyebrow in question. Eve doesn't stop to consider; indeed the decision to sleep with another woman was made weeks ago. It's only the focus that has changed. She stands and sheds her clothes with the economical movements she uses at home. There's no seduction in undressing with Teri, it's merely something she does before bed. When she unhooks her bra, she pauses. She's been naked with other women, of course—in the gym, at the doctor's office for the impersonality of medical exams, and once in a giggly drunken riot of skinny-dipping women after an evening out—but this is the first time in years she's undressed in front of someone in a sexual way. She feels she should slow it down, add some allure to the process.

Justine rises and stops her hands. Her lips trace a line down Eve's collarbone, down to where the bra cuts a satin line across her flesh. Justine's lips close over Eve's nipple through the bra, the damp suction shooting arrows down her belly. Her bra falls away—when had Justine unhooked it?—and then Justine's mouth is on Eve's naked flesh, teasing her nipples into hard points.

Eve focuses on the moment, on the way Justine's mouth is making her feel, on the dampness of her panties against her cunt, on the throb and pulse of her clit. Justine is still dressed, but when Eve moves her hands to the buttons of Justine's shirt, the dark woman shrugs her aside, drops to her knees and presses her mouth to the crotch of Eve's panties. Eve lightly trimmed her bush for this evening—it's not something she usually does, but, aware of current trends, she didn't want her luxuriant curls to be a turn-off. She must smell musky down there, even through the satin of her panties, but Justine presses her face closer, pulls the gusset to one side, and traces the outline of her pussy with her tongue.

There's a bucking bronco of sensations riding in Eve's stomach. A stranger's touch. Teri knows what she likes, but Justine is learning as she goes. She's not tentative in her movements, but it's the wrong sort of friction for Eve. She likes it on the side of her clit, she needs a steady pressure, she has to have rhythm, not this touch, withdraw, touch, withdraw that Justine's doing. But then Justine tickles a circle with her tongue, and Teri flies out of Eve's head, and what she likes is being redrawn with each movement of Justine's tongue.

There's white noise in her head, and when she closes her eyes there's a whole universe behind them. This is what she wanted. Her stomach clenches and she thinks she's going to come, and suddenly she's scared at how instantly she's aroused, how urgent the pressure and how she's going to peak in only a few minutes, when it normally takes longer. She opens her eyes, and her knees shake. The sight of Justine's dark body on the floor in front of her, face between her legs, is overwhelming, and she sits abruptly on the edge of the bed and removes her panties with trembling hands.

Justine rises, sheds her clothes, and crawls up alongside her. "Touch me," she commands.

Eve's fingers want to fall into familiar patterns, but she halts them with conscious effort. Instead, she bends and takes Justine's nipple deep into her mouth, swirling and sucking. She bites lightly. Justine's answering arch of her back, pushing her breast deeper into Eve's mouth, is her reward.

She concentrates on the newness, the sensations, the differences. Justine's skin is springy over hard muscle. There's resilience to her body, a lack of fragility in her limbs, a robustness that seems to come from within. Eve's used to leading, but as she's learning the contours of Justine's body—biceps, dimples, curves, planes and the places in between, like highways to be traversed between attractions, Justine takes her hand and shoves it between her thighs, as if she's impatient to get to the climax.

Eve's fingers still. This is the part that will take her to hell, this is where there is no coy evasion about motives, or intent. This is where the evening has been going, and this is the moment where there is really no going back. She can feel the heat and slickness and this is what she has wanted, what she's risking everything for. She explores, mapping the contours of a different pussy, learning the shape of puffy outer lips, of slick inner folds, learning that one woman is as different from another as night and day. When her finger pushes inside, as she adds a second, she falls into the pattern of strokes that Teri likes.

Justine raises a thigh so that Eve has better access. Eve looks at her hand, how it rests against a different pussy, the dark crinkly hair that is so harsh against her hand. The allure of the forbidden steals her breath momentarily. She pistons her fingers, watching Justine's face, the tiny movements that signal her delight. This level of concentration on the act is strange for Eve; something that normally is a welter of learned moves is now tentative.

Justine holds Eve's wrist and directs her movements, with nudges, and encouragement in her voice. "There, honey, a little faster, a little harder, oh, honey, now you've got it." There's an authoritarian tone to her voice, like a schoolteacher explaining something for the first time, but Eve ignores it. When it's her turn, she resolves, she will be just as direct.

Justine's orgasm is an explosion of sound, a flurry of movement, as her voice keens in pleasure and her hips shudder and jolt. Her pussy clamps hard on Eve's fingers, and in delight, Eve feels the internal shivers and spasms.

This is what it feels like, she thinks, these are the sounds, the smell, the taste, the joy of sex with someone else.

Justine rises onto her elbows. "You're a fast learner, honey. Your Teri is a lucky woman."

At the mention of Teri's name some of the pleasure seeps from Eve's head. But she pushes the thought away, as she needs to taste, and her own clit is throbbing an insistent rhythm for release. She bends, puts her mouth to Justine's cunt and tastes. She's not trying to make her come again, this is for her, to know the sensation of another pussy on her tongue. Justine is spicy-sweet, and her juices are thicker than Eve is used to. She pushes her tongue inside the other woman's cunt, eager to experience.

Justine lets her for a few moments—maybe she remembers their conversation of earlier—before she pushes her away, and in a quick reversal, Eve is on her back on the bed, Justine kneeling over her.

"How d'you want it, honey? I have long fingers and an agile tongue."

The buzz of expectation is back. "Both," says Eve, in a voice dry with need, "fuck me with your fingers, suck me with your mouth."

Justine pushes her thighs so wide apart Eve feels she might split. She is open, exposed, and the way Justine studies her is unnerving. But then Justine kisses each nipple, and her mouth works downward, over Eve's belly, down to where the curls start. Eve is wet, and her breath comes in thick pants of anticipation. Justine's fingers outline Eve's cunt lips, and then with one push she slips two fingers deep inside. Her lips descend, and she sucks Eve's clit with her whole mouth. It's different from before, different from anything Teri does, it's rough and it's raw, and it overwhelms Eve. The evening coalesces in her head, a blur of euphoria, anger, disappointment and lust. It's like a patchwork of weeks shoved together into the space of a few hours. So when her orgasm rises as fast as a hurricane and just as fierce, she goes with it, riding the tide, letting it buffet her, letting it wash the guilt and worry from her head and replace them with the immediateness and physicality of the moment.

*Now I know,* she thinks, in the aftermath of the storm, as Justine wipes her mouth, and presses a kiss to her belly. *This is what another woman is like.*

After Justine has left, Eve lies on the bed that smells of sex, with her hands behind her head, and although she's watching the ball game on TV, she's thinking of home.

Teri and Murphy come barreling out of the shabby ranch house before the car has come to a halt. The weak sun paints Teri's eager face with warmth and Eve looks at her as if for the first time, sees her tip-tilted eyes, the curve of her cheek with the downy hairs Teri hates catching the sunlight. She is beautiful.

"How did it go? Did you get the contract?" Teri runs to the car, Murphy on her heels, and pulls the door open.

Eve blinks at her, stupidly. Contract? Her brain connects

once more and she remembers the lies she spun as the reason for the trip to Denver. She has to swallow hard, once, twice, before she can trust her voice. "I don't think so. I think they thought we were a bigger operation."

The words she rehearsed as she drove up I-25 have evaporated into the mist in her brain and all she can think of is how much she loves Teri. She thinks of their bed, and how they lie there together, Murphy on their feet taking up too much room, and she longs for the taste of Teri's mouth, the delicate shiver of her pale skin, the hot clasp of her pussy.

She thinks of all she found so mundane, before Denver, and now it seems so fragile and wondrous, something to be treasured. Eve exits the car, and holds out her arms. Teri walks into them, and Eve realizes that it will be all right, that Teri doesn't—can't—know.

She kisses Teri, pushes her hands into her short hair, holds her close, and rocks her. "I missed you so much," she murmurs and the words are the truest thing she's ever said.

"Told you I should have come too." Teri settles her face against Eve's shoulder, and sighs. "Murph and I really missed you."

Eve holds her lover and thinks about all that she could lose if Teri were ever to find out. For she will hold the secret now, afraid of slipping, afraid of what its revelation could bring. Already it sits in her stomach, in the back of her throat, a hard ball of words threatening to break free.

Eve pushes the words away and holds Teri close, settling into her lover, all that they have been together, and all that they can be.

# THE FURTHER ADVENTURES OF MISS SCARLET

Emily L. Byrne

Kendra could almost feel someone's eyes burning a hole in the back of her head. She didn't even need to turn around to confirm the feeling, thanks to the mirror over the bar. If it had been any other bar, she would have been more surprised. But Riley's was a cop bar and it attracted a specific clientele, mostly law enforcement and their families and friends. Plus the occasional groupie.

Whatever this woman was, she wasn't law enforcement, at least not any kind that Kendra had seen before. Or could imagine. She was beautiful: heart-shaped face, arched thin eyebrows over wide dark eyes, bright-red kissable lips. Her red dress set off her curves, accentuating her small, full breasts and curved hips, even sitting down. And what was she looking at? A big African American butch with dreads, a broken nose and shoulders like a linebacker's. For a minute, Kendra wished with everything she had that she was cuter, and bit back a sigh.

But that moment passed; she was cute enough to stare at, so that was as cute as she needed to be. At least for now. She could turn her attention to wishing she were less shy around pretty ladies instead. That wish settled down into her crotch with a dull, aching thud of thwarted desire. It had been way too long, and she was uncertain and out of practice.

She was entertaining herself by covertly studying the other woman's reflection, trying to figure out if she'd run across her before and could use that as a conversation starter, when her partner nudged her. "Got yourself a badge bunny, Ken? Not too shabby." James grinned as she turned and wrinkled her nose at him. He took a swig of his beer and glanced around the rest of the bar as if her potential romantic drama held no more interest for him.

It probably didn't. James would finish his beer and head home to his wife and kids, just like he did every Thursday night. In the times between his one weekly night out and his biweekly card games, he mowed his lawn, played with his kids and stayed home as much as he could. And worked with Kendra to solve homicides the rest of the time.

Though, come to think of it, that last part was more than enough drama for Kendra, too. She found her eyes wandering back to the mirror anyway. The woman had disappeared and she stifled another sigh. There had been something intriguing, challenging even, in the other woman's stare. It had been a while since anyone had challenged Detective Kendra McClain, and she hadn't realized how much she'd missed it until now.

Disappointed, she called it a night, said goodbye to James and the others and left the bar. She let her steps take her toward the subway while her mind wandered back to the woman in red. She had a weird sense that she'd seen that same woman, or someone who looked like her, before.

The fact that she couldn't place her bothered Kendra. It wasn't like she knew that many beautiful women of Asian descent. She didn't know very many beautiful women, period. And certainly not any who would stare at her like that.

She imagined the other woman in her bed for a wild moment,

tan skin silky under her hands, the woman's long black hair cascading over both of them like a veil. Her wet, warm flesh parting around Kendra's hands. The detective bit her lip, her skin on fire, her body one giant, quivering nerve ending that ached with longing.

Clearly, it had been way too long.

Kendra drew a shaky breath and walked down the subway stairs, grateful for the cool night air on her cheeks and the fact that the stairs were deserted at this hour. If she was blushing, at least there'd be no one around to see it. She smiled to herself as she entered the dimly lit corridor that led to the ticket booth.

Then her instincts took over. Something was wrong. She caught a flash of red at the end of the corridor. Someone either turned or ducked back around the corner, like they were hiding from her. Kendra moved her hand closer to the gun in her jacket and kept walking, all senses alert and focused. A quick glance at the booth told her that it was unoccupied, so she'd need her pass to get through the gate to the station platform. And there'd be no one to call for backup if she needed it.

She paused for a moment. Maybe she should backtrack and go to another entrance. More trouble was no way to end an already stressful week. She could always call the Transit Police when she got back up the stairs. That was when another flash of red caught her eye. This time, though, she could see that it looked like a red dress. A familiar red dress.

Kendra frowned; this was one coincidence too many. What if this woman, whoever she was, wasn't alone? She might be walking into a trap. It might not even be the woman from the bar. But her curiosity, leavened with a bit of residual lust, overrode her common sense. Instead of turning back, she loped forward, dashing around the corner to catch whoever was waiting for her by surprise.

But the station looked empty from where she was standing. She cursed quietly and pulled out her pass. A train rumbled in the distance and for a moment, she wondered if she was letting her imagination run away with her, fantasizing about strange women in her bed and then stalking her for good measure.

She stepped out onto the platform and looked around. The woman from the bar was sitting on a nearby bench, seemingly engrossed in an e-reader. Then she slowly crossed one long, lithe leg over the other, displaying them to full advantage in the latest fashion in stilettos. She shifted on the bench just a hair, giving her back a tiny arch. The movement was clearly an invitation and Kendra went over to sit next to her.

The other woman ignored her, but she twisted one lock of hair around her finger and Kendra could see her white teeth chewing her scarlet lower lip. Something about the way she did it went straight to Kendra's crotch. If she licked those lips, the detective knew that she was doomed.

"Didn't I see you at Riley's Pub tonight?" Kendra tried to make her tone sound innocent, like every inch of her body wasn't stirring to a slow, fierce arousal.

The other woman tilted her face up to look at Kendra and the detective had the nervous urge to straighten her dreads and check her teeth for scraps of food. She was every bit as beautiful as her reflection in the bar mirror: dark eyes above high cheek-bones, kissable full lips, low-cut dress showing more than a hint of cleavage.

Her expression was anything but welcoming, though, and that detached, even icy look triggered a memory in the back of Kendra's mind. She knew where she'd seen that face before, knew that it was something to do with another department's case. But which one? Not a homicide. That much, at least, she was sure of. Hopefully.

"Yes, detective. You did see me at Riley's." The woman's voice was a purr, stroking its way up Kendra's thighs. "I'm glad that you found me so...memorable." Her lips curled in a smile that didn't make it up to her eyes.

Kendra's brain murmured words like "drama" and "trouble" and "potential criminal" while her pussy sang a different song entirely. "You certainly seemed to want me to notice you. What's your name?"

The smile widened, brilliant lipstick parting over bright white teeth. "You can call me Scarlet, Miss Scarlet, if we're going to be formal." She tucked the e-reader away in a small black bag that matched her heels, but she didn't take her gaze away from Kendra's face.

"Are we playing Clue? I'm not sure I want to be Colonel Mustard in the library, with or without a candlestick." Kendra grimaced. She glanced down, this time looking beyond Scarlet's body to her accessories. James always said that you could read a lot about a woman by what kind of jewelry she wore and how she put together her outfits. Kendra usually blew that off as his one concession to metrosexuality, but she was willing to make an exception tonight.

Everything matched, not a hair out of place, not a chipped nail or a makeup smudge. Everything this woman wore was assembled with such care and thoroughness that she might have been playing a part onstage. With one exception: one of her rings was a giant, gaudy bit of bling that didn't match her industrial-style silver earrings, necklace and watch. The ring was a mass of ornate curlicues around a faceted glass stone that was far too large and shiny to be a real diamond.

"Nice ring," Kendra drawled as the station signal beeped to let them know that their train was coming in.

"Like it?" Scarlet smiled at her upraised hand. "I—" The noise of the onrushing train cut her off. But for one crazy moment, Kendra could have sworn that she said, "I stole two others nearly the same size in Monte Carlo last year."

"What?" Kendra looked at Scarlet as closely as she could as she trailed the other woman onto the train. She reached for her phone, wondering if she could do a quick search on jewel thefts in Monte Carlo without arousing too much suspicion. But they were alone in the train car and headed into a tunnel, so there would be no signal even if she tried to manage a text message.

They were sitting down and Scarlet was resting her hand on Kendra's arm, caressing it, stroking it until Kendra, watching it, thought she might go up in flames. "You're so very strong, detective. I do like a nice strong girl." Scarlet looked up at her through thick black lashes, her gaze an invitation.

A tiny bit of Kendra's remaining common sense prompted her to ask, "How did you know that I'm a detective? Maybe I'm just out of uniform." Scarlet's hand was on her thigh now, and common sense was becoming very hard to come by. Self-control was going to be next. Kendra hoped that she wasn't actually panting.

Scarlet smiled at her. "I saw you on TV when the mayor commended you and your partner. I pay a lot of attention to the police force. You could say that they're terribly important to me. And you were such a stud up there on the podium that I couldn't resist tracking you down. Do I scare you, detective? I wouldn't want you to have to use those cuffs on me." She watched Kendra through lowered eyelashes, her expression schoolgirl demure and about as real.

It was an invitation that Kendra couldn't ignore. She reached over, tilted the other woman's chin up and kissed her. Then Scarlet's hand was wrapped around her neck and buried in her hair and Scarlet's tongue was in her mouth. She tasted like piña coladas, expensive lipstick and lust and Kendra responded to all three, picking her up and swinging her onto her lap so that the other woman knelt on the seat with her thighs on either side of the detective's. Scarlet wriggled up close to Kendra, pressing her lithe body against the detective's and shoving one of Kendra's hands up under her skirt.

Kendra held back a moan and a moment of panic. Transit police or more passengers could enter the car at any moment.

This was nuts. She didn't know this woman, and even suspected her of being a criminal. This had to stop...but her hand had developed a will of its own and was stroking Scarlet's thigh. Her smooth, silky thigh above her lacy garter belt. Kendra deliberately stopped her hand just shy of Scarlet's panties, ignoring the other woman's efforts to pull her hand farther up.

Instead, she broke off their kiss, running her tongue down Scarlet's neck and gently nipping her shoulder. Part of her brain noted that they were pulling into a station, and she adjusted them a little bit so that what they had been on the brink of doing was slightly less obvious. Scarlet's mouth was at her ear, her teeth nibbling her earlobe. Her voice in Kendra's ear whispered urgently, "Oh c'mon, detective! If someone gets on, let's give them a show. I like an audience for my performances. Don't you?"

She shifted her body on top of Kendra's and ground her hips against the detective's. The wave of pure desire that swept over Kendra just then made it hard to talk, to tell this woman that, no, she never made love with an audience. And the thought of doing it was revolting and gross. And unbelievably hot.

Then Scarlet's hand was under her jacket, kneading her breast and tugging her nipple into an excruciating point and who needed to think right now?

With a growl, she buried her face in Scarlet's cleavage, biting and licking every bit of bare skin she could reach from that angle. Scarlet yanked one of her small breasts free of her bra's lacy cups, holding it up with her fingertips so that Kendra could engulf it with her mouth, sucking and nibbling until she could feel the other woman's groan start at her toes and work its way up.

She gave up her struggle to hold her hand still, instead letting it slide up Scarlet's thigh to her soaking wet panties. She ran her fingers over them, gratified at the abrupt tilt of the other woman's hips that followed her movements. "Inside me, detective. C'mon, baby. You going to make me beg?" Scarlet murmured the words in her ear, her voice caressing enough to call up a full body shiver.

It would be tempting to see what this woman could do if she was really begging for it. Kendra grinned into the sharp point of the nipple that she held clenched lightly between her front teeth. But then, turnabout might be fair play. Kendra twitched a little at the thought of what she'd be willing to do to get this woman to say yes to her. And act on it.

She sent her fingers up and around Scarlet's panties, until she could bury them into the wet welcome that awaited her on the other side of the satin barrier. Scarlet moaned and humped her hand, rocking forward to take in as much of Kendra's hand as she could. It was so sweet, this beautiful woman's desire, so novel and lovely, that it was almost enough to shut off the detective part of Kendra's brain.

But not quite. On autopilot, her brain ran through everything she'd done and seen at the station recently, cataloging and searching her memories as she was trained to do, looking for the one that would tell her why Scarlet looked familiar.

What came back was a photo on a case file that she'd seen some colleagues passing around at a meeting. "Interpol says she's one of the best they've ever seen. And my buddy says she's hotter than hell, even better than her picture. The cops in Macao and Monte Carlo and everywhere else on the effin' planet are looking for her. Maybe we'll get lucky and she'll come here next." The conversation had trailed off into chest-thumping commentary about what they'd like to do with a gorgeous female jewel thief and Kendra had tuned them out. It wouldn't be her case unless the woman killed someone, so what did she care?

The tensing of Scarlet's thighs overrode her thoughts as she brought the other woman to orgasm right there on the train, just as it entered a new station. Head tilted back, red lips parted in a series of moans and cries, Scarlet had given herself up to the moment, and Kendra wanted that moment to last. Maybe she was wrong about who this woman was. Why would a world-class jewel thief go slumming at Riley's to pick up a detective, after all?

Then Scarlet's lips fastened on hers, her tongue so urgent that wrestling with it, added to the press of Scarlet's body on hers, was enough to drive any other thoughts from her head. She barely noticed that they weren't alone in the car anymore. She did finally open one eyelid, just a slit, and verified that the couple who'd gotten on were sitting far enough away not to pose an immediate threat. Kendra was willing to take that for now.

Or at least she was until Scarlet began wedging her hand down her pants. "We've got an audience," she growled, breaking off the kiss and moving to intercept those enticingly long fingers, now suddenly ringless. *Where did it go? It might be evidence.*

"Let them watch. We'll show them how it's done," Scarlet whispered and ran her tongue down Kendra's neck. "You've got a gun to hold them off if they want to participate. I don't like sharing." Scarlet gave her a satiated half smile, like a happy cat's, and tweaked her nipple, pulling a suffocated moan from Kendra's closed lips. "I'll keep an eye on them. Let me finish what we started, detective. Trust me."

Kendra's instincts all woke up. Could she really trust this woman? How far? At least the train tunnels would block enough Wi-Fi signals that they probably wouldn't end up on YouTube if the car's other occupants had cell phones. Probably.

Scarlet took advantage of the lapse in Kendra's attention to shove her hand down her pants and Kendra felt her hips rock forward to make more room for her, her body responding as if it belonged to someone else. Scarlet, perhaps. Not that she'd be able to relax enough to come, not here and now. She was certain of that much.

But Scarlet's fingers said something entirely different as they slid into her and one finger found her clit. Kendra jumped a little at the shock of the sudden, longed-for contact and Scarlet leaned down to kiss her again, her exposed breast rubbing against Kendra's until the detective wondered if she could slip her T-shirt off under her jacket. She wanted to be naked with this woman so badly, she wasn't sure that the location mattered anymore.

"Just me. Just my hand and your pussy. That's all that matters. Give me what you want to give so badly," Scarlet crooned as she covered her face with little kisses. "I can feel how much you want to come for me, baby. Let me get you there." The pressure of her fingers increased, sending a spark of pure fire through Kendra, circling and pushing in just the right amount.

Kendra's brain disintegrated into a jumbled mass of fantasies, all of them about this gorgeous woman and all the things she wanted to do with her. But the weight of hungry eyes was making her anxious. Well, that and the possibility that Interpol was looking for her companion. What was a good detective to do?

She risked a quick glance down the car. The straight couple was watching them, but their hands were so busy that they'd have other things to occupy them soon. Part of her cringed at providing a free show for them. "Just us, baby. They're only trying to have as much fun as we are. Show them how it's done." Scarlet's voice cut across her thoughts and fears as she kissed her eyelids closed, shutting out their watchers.

She could feel Scarlet's hips thrust against hers, feel the urgency in her breathing and the rapid pounding of her heart. She let it carry her away, shutting away everything except this woman and her maddening, exciting touch. Her thighs locked instinctively and tightened until all of her being centered on that single point of fire being coaxed into unbearable sensitivity. A moment, a breath, and someone was shouting, the sound muted by the train screeching around a corner.

When Kendra came back to earth, Scarlet was grinning at

her and licking her fingers, a sight that sent a stab of soft fire through the detective. "My, my. I knew you'd be hot, baby." Scarlet leaned over and kissed her hard as she tucked herself back into her bra and pulled her dress closed.

"Come home with me," Kendra murmured as Scarlet tucked her shirt back in. "I'm even more fun horizontal. Or vertical, if you prefer."

Scarlet swung off her as the guy from the other end of the car approached. "We were wondering if...you two were, um, bi-curious?" He stopped a few feet away, like he expected to get punched if he got too close. It was a good idea on his part; Kendra was considering the option, hard.

Scarlet gave him a twisted grin. "Not tonight. Or probably any night thereafter. I think your lady's got enough to fuel her imagination for quite a while to come as it is." She waved him off and he turned and went back to his date, keeping any growling he wanted to do about his dismissal to himself.

"That happen every time you have sex on trains?" Kendra glanced sidelong at Scarlet, her mood turning dark as her brain warred with her body. At the very least, she needed a closer look at the ring. A memory of a certain sparkle crossed her mind, and she couldn't shed the suspicion that she'd heard Scarlet correctly back at the station.

"Haven't done this before. Not in this city at least. But I always like to try something new in a new town. Souvenirs are some of the best parts of any trip, aren't they, detective?" Scarlet's smile had turned wistful.

Then she gave Kendra a speculative look, and rose slowly, tugging at her dress to straighten it out. She glanced up as if to see what station they were pulling into and Kendra glanced over her own shoulder. Only two more stops to her apartment. She wondered what, if anything, she could say to get Scarlet back there. Though maybe exposing a suspected thief to her meager possessions wasn't the best idea.

But she couldn't let her get away, no matter what. She gathered herself to reach for Scarlet as the doors opened.

There was a familiar flash of red on the platform and Kendra realized her pants weren't fastened any more. She grabbed them with a curse as the doors closed. Scarlet stood on the platform and blew her a kiss. She tapped her shoulder as the train pulled out of the station and after a moment, Kendra realized that she was supposed to check her jacket pocket. There was something hard in it, something that hadn't been there at the beginning of this crazy night.

The ring was heavy and solid in her hand, the stone sparkling in a way that confirmed her suspicions. She gingerly placed it on the subway window glass and used it to make a tiny scratch. *Shit.* Was it a memento? Or was the other woman trying to frame her? But that didn't make sense. All she had to do was to turn it in and say she'd found it on the subway and wondered if there was a report out on it.

She pocketed the ring and contemplated taking a cab back to the previous stop. But Scarlet would be long gone by then. She knew that in her gut. Her aching, empty gut. Kendra rested her head against the cold glass and watched the dark walls of the tunnel blur by until the train pulled into her stop.

It was only when she was trudging up the stairs that she realized Scarlet had been telling her that she'd be sticking around for a little while. Maybe the ring was a goodwill gesture as well as a souvenir. Maybe Scarlet would come looking for her again.

Or maybe she needed to concentrate on being a cop and take a closer look at the other woman's file to see what she could find out. One way or another, she hadn't seen the last of Miss Scarlet.

She held her fingers up to her nose and inhaled the other woman's scent, grinning despite herself. Detective Kendra McClain liked a challenge and it looked like she was in luck. Kendra whistled as she headed home, checking for a flash of red dress around every corner.

# ABOUT THE AUTHORS

**VALERIE ALEXANDER** lives in Los Angeles. Her work has previously been published in *Best of Best Women's Erotica, The Big Book of Domination, Best Lesbian Erotica* and other anthologies.

**LOUISE BLAYDON** is a writer and academic who loves cats too much. She writes m/m and f/f fiction primarily, but has been known to dabble. She lives in the country with an ever-increasing number of pets.

**HARPER BLISS** is a lesbian fiction author of romantic and erotic stories with varying degrees of hotness. She lives on an outlying island in Hong Kong with her wife and, regrettably, zero pets.

**CHEYENNE BLUE's** (cheyenneblue.com) erotic fiction has been included in over ninety anthologies since 2000. She is the editor of *Forbidden Fruit: Stories of Unwise Lesbian Desire*. She now writes, runs, makes bread and cheese and drinks wine by the beach in Queensland, Australia.

**EMILY L. BYRNE** (writeremilylbyrne.blogspot.com) lives in lovely Minneapolis with her wife and the two cats that own them. She toils in corporate IT by day, and writes as much of the rest of the time as possible.

**SOSSITY CHIRICUZIO** (sossitywrites.com) is a queer femme outlaw poet, a working-class sex radical storyteller—what her friends' parents often referred to as a bad influence, and possibly still do. A 2015 Lambda Fellow, her recent publications include: *Adrienne, Wilde, Glitterwolf, Salacious, Say Please* and *Leather Ever After.*

**R. G. EMANUELLE's** (rgemanuelle.com) published works include *Twice Bitten, Add Spice to Taste* and short stories in numerous anthologies. She coedited the Lambda Award Finalist anthology *All You Can Eat: A Buffet of Lesbian Erotica & Romance,* as well as *Unwrap These Presents* and *Skulls and Crossbones.*

**ROSE DE FER's** stories have appeared in *Best Women's Erotica 2014, The Mammoth Book of Erotic Romance & Domination, Hungry for More, The Big Book of Submission, Red Velvet & Absinthe, Darker Edge of Desire, A Princess Bound* and numerous Mischief anthologies including *Underworlds, Submission* and *Forever Bound.* She lives in England.

**FRANKIE GRAYSON,** a longtime lover of the literary dark arts, is thrilled that her first published erotic story is with *Best Lesbian Erotica: 20th Anniversary Edition.* More to come.

**D. L. KING** (dlkingerotica.blogspot.com), is the editor of the Lambda Literary Award winner and gold medalist, *The Harder She Comes,* Lammy Finalist *Where the Girls Are,* and *She Who Must Be Obeyed: Femme Dominant Lesbian Erotica,* among others. Find her in various editions of *Best Lesbian Erotica*, and many other titles.

**ANNABETH LEONG** (annabetherotica.com) is frequently confused about her sexuality but enjoys searching for answers. Her work appears in dozens of anthologies, including *Summer Love: Lesbian Stories of Holiday Romance*. She is the author of the butch-femme BDSM novella *Heated Leather Lover*.

**ROSE P. LETHE** is a corporate copyeditor, copywriter, and watcher of cat videos. After completing an MFA in creative writing, she found she could no longer stomach "serious literature" and has since turned to more enjoyable creative pursuits.

**MEGAN MCFERREN** enjoys exploring queer history through erotic romance, and illuminating the love that once dared not speak its name. Texan by birth and New Yorker by choice, she has contributed stories to anthologies from Torquere Press and The Liz McMullen Show Publications.

**JEAN ROBERTA** (jeanroberta.com) teaches English and creative writing in a Canadian university. She writes erotica, fantasy, historical fiction, drama, poetry and nonfiction. She channeled Dr. Athena Chalkdust in *Best Lesbian Erotica 2001, 2005,* and *2009*.

**TERESA NOELLE ROBERTS** started writing stories in kindergarten, and she hasn't stopped yet. A prolific author of short erotica, she's also a published poet and fantasy writer. BDSM-spiced contemporary romances, hot paranormals and spicy science fiction romances are her favorite novels to write. When not writing, she gardens like a fiend.

**SINCLAIR SEXSMITH** (sugarbutch.net) is a genderqueer kinky butch writer who teaches and performs, specializing in sexualities, genders and relationships. Sinclair's gender theory and queer erotica is widely published, and they edited *Best Lesbian Erotica 2012* and *Say Please: Lesbian BDSM Erotica*, and wrote *Sweet & Rough: Sixteen Stories of Queer Smut*.

**ANNA WATSON** is a piece of tired-ass pimento baloney in the white bread sandwich of her teenage sons and elderly parents, and yet she bravely soldiers on, writing and publishing as much butch/femme smut as possible. She's pretty sure she deserves a femme medal of valor, and is just waiting for the awarding body to appear.

# ABOUT THE EDITOR

SACCHI GREEN is a writer and editor of erotica and other stimulating genres. Her stories have appeared in scores of publications, including eight volumes of *Best Lesbian Erotica*, four of *Best Women's Erotica*, five of *Best Lesbian Romance*, *Best Transgender Erotica*, *Best Fantasy Erotica* and *Penthouse*. In recent years she's taken to wielding the editorial whip, editing ten lesbian erotica anthologies including *Lesbian Cowboys*, *Girl Crazy*, *Lesbian Lust*, *Women with Handcuffs*, *Girl Fever* and *Wild Girls, Wild Nights,* all from Cleis Press, and *Thunder of War, Lightning of Desire* (Lethe Press). Five have been Lambda Literary Award Finalists, and two, *Lesbian Cowboys* and *Wild Girls, Wild Nights,* have been Lambda winners. A collection of her own work, *A Ride to Remember* from Lethe Press, was also a Lambda Finalist.

Sacchi can be found online at sacchi-green.blogspot.com and Facebook. In her corporeal form she resides in western Massachusetts, with frequent getaways to a cabin in the White Mountains of New Hampshire and occasional forays into the real world.

Printed in the United States
By Bookmasters